DYSTOPIAN GIRLS

By Rodzil LaBraun

CHAPTER ONE:

I was checking all the cupboards in the recently remodeled kitchen when I heard a ruckus in the backyard. It was almost dark, much later in the day than I usually went foraging. My desire for some kind of processed pastry drove me out of my comfort zone this evening. Leaning over the stainless-steel kitchen sink I peered out the double pane window in search of what may have created the disturbance. I saw nothing and heard even less, so after a minute of holding my breath I figured it must have been a rodent or the like.

This classy contemporary kitchen had evidently been picked through previously. The solid oak doors and drawers were already open. A variety of undesired items and wrappers of consumed food were scattered on the marble tile floor. Marble? Really? Probably not. This neighborhood was nice, but not that nice. Still, the floor looked expensive and remained shiny from its last mopping.

Of course, there were no packaged cupcakes or similar treats. I knew from experience that the hunger for a sugary pastry would pass in time, but I was physically compelled to search until then. This house on Norcross Way was too obvious of a target to continue to hold anything of value. In the weeks since the global catastrophe, so many private homes had been ravaged by individuals bent on survival. Grocery and convenience stores were much better supply stations, but they were often occupied by gangs. I still can't shake the memory of seeing that defenseless woman brutally murdered in the bread aisle. That was back before the viruses spread like wildfire and there were much more people still alive. Guilt for not trying to help her plagued my soul, but I would have just ended up dead alongside of her.

Finally giving up on the food hunt, I checked the obvious locations for more batteries and bottled water. Better yet would be anything that could purify water more effectively than the filtered pitcher I was currently using. Ever since the plumbing stopped working, clean drinking water was the highest priority. Electricity was still missed, but not nearly as required for survival as I once believed. The internet stopped working even before that, and the news it provided was the only thing of importance. The time for selfies, likes and shares had long passed. I always believed people's obsession with social media was a bit immature, but now it seems absurdly ridiculous.

Okay, nothing left to gleam here. Time to head back across New Hampshire Avenue to my place before it gets too dark to make out predators. The six-lane highway was once a busy artery of suburban traffic. Now it is just a big open space where you could be vulnerable to attack from a variety of sources, man or animal. It had been weeks since I heard the sound of a motored vehicle. I assumed gasoline was in extremely short supply. Once people started dropping like flies, I shied away from anything that would get me noticed, like the combustion engine of a car or truck. Of course, escaping notice had kind of been my thing all along. Though an only child, I never really sought attention. All my athletic endeavors had nothing to do with getting noticed. It was really more of a self-worth kind of thing. I think.

Well, anyway, there I stood at the front door of the two-story brick home that I had been searching. The skillfully engraved, heavy oak door was hanging awkwardly from its brass hinges. Not my doing. I found it that way. Surprisingly, the flimsy metal storm door was still intact, though not closing properly. The glass had been slid down so only the screen was present up top. I stood there, as was my custom, listening and searching visibly for any red flags outside before I exit. Caution these days could make the difference between life and death. The few people that I had befriended since the world ended did not fully grasp that concept, unfortunately. They carelessly got themselves killed before I could really consider them a friend, or even a travel companion.

It was that shocking loss of life that discouraged me from roaming as much as I had previously. I spent much of my time these days hunkered down in the concrete building of the old Hollywood Beer & Wine store. It's structure and limited access made it easily defended against most foes. Each day I would try to improve its fortification and comfort. There were still some edible food items in the deli section and storeroom, but a lot of rotten meat needed to be tossed in the charred dumpster out back. It drew animals for a while, but none were able to get into the store, so that was okay.

I had a cot set up behind the cashier's counter and blocked all the doors and windows sufficiently for safety. That left the place dreadfully dark all the time, so lantern batteries were a daily necessity. The lack of sufficient air flow produced an oven effect. There was no longer a working air conditioner anywhere without electricity. A gas generator could solve that problem, but for how long? And would I get myself killed siphoning gasoline on a regular basis? I decided I might as well get used to living on the basics, since there was no reason to expect improvement in this world in the foreseeable future.

Movement caught my eye to the left, and I ducked down hoping that I had not already been noticed. Shortly thereafter, a limping mangy excuse for a female human wandered across the front lawn. Though I could not smell her from my hiding spot, I knew that it was a skank. That is what Ashley had called them before she got herself killed by a few. They were people that physically decayed from the viruses, but never died. Their mental capacity appeared to be limited as they focused mostly on finding their next meal. They were cannibals, trash eaters, and nasty fuckers in every sense. Ashley called the girls skanks and the guys skunks. The name fit and I continued to use it even after her death. Of course, most of my conversation was with myself. Even stray dogs didn't stick around long.

The skank stopped abruptly on the stone sidewalk that led from the street to the front door where I was hidden and made a barking type noise. It was their communication and resembled the English language occasionally. Two more skanks appeared to the left and followed their stinky friend into the front yard. Then another came from the right to begin a meeting of rotten walking flesh blocking my exit. This one was a skunk I could tell from his scraggly beard and wife-beater undershirt exposing a flat chest. He was probably something like a leader for the hungry gang. The vast majority of survivors, I noticed, were female. The rare male would easily gain respect in this new dystopian world that he might not otherwise deserve.

I drew in a quick breath when one of the skanks motioned toward the house where I crouched in the shadow of the doorway. Then another gestured across the street and seemed to convince the others that they should shuffle their sorry asses that way. Appreciative, I watched the pathetic group effort as they headed for a burnt brick home that looked very similar to this one. One skank fell twice, tripping over the curb the first time, then something invisible the next. The skunk kicked her after the second time and the other skanks barked and pointed. I realize then that it was laughter. Perhaps these sub-humans maintained more of their humanity than I realized.

The group continued their disjointed journey. The injured female only fell behind enough to keep from getting kicked again. Eventually, they disappeared behind the house and I became conscious of the fact that all my focus had been on the stinky gang. I failed to keep my eyes and ears open for other threats. I needed to reassess the safety of the house first, then watch out front again for a few minutes.

My extra caution was rewarded when I witnessed two more forms enter the street. These were both female but walked with more coordination and strength than the nasty skanks. They also carried weapons. Both had golf clubs, and one carried a sword. I imagined it had been pried off the living room wall of some abandoned home, then fought over several times in the sad feudal weeks that followed. The current owner was carrying it unsheathed and making aggressive cutting motions in the air before her. Her partner widened the space between them, showing some good sense, as they appeared to follow the other gang around the house. Were they skank hunters? What could they possibly gain from chasing down the nasty group? They wouldn't even be good eating, if you were so inclined. They had no possessions to steal. But it didn't matter really. All I cared about was that they weren't coming after me.

Staying in the shadows as best I could, I slowly made my way back the short cul-de-sac street toward the main road. My concrete fortress was visible in the dim twilight from there. The trash I propped in front of the entrance looked to be undisturbed since I left. That was good. I was not in the mood for guests. I took a couple more minutes to observe the open area of New Hampshire Avenue. The street originated in Washington DC and was named after a state like so many other streets in the nation's capital. Then it extended way out into the country. Some undamaged street signs were visible, surprisingly. There were also a few abandoned cars, but not many. The catastrophe that befell our planet did not happen overnight. Most people died in their homes or in hospitals. Their cars were properly parked between painted lines or in a driveway before they realized how bad things were going to be.

Nothing to see here, so I jogged quietly across the pavement and concrete median to duck behind a pickup truck parked in the beer store parking lot. If my movement caught anyone's attention, I would like to know that now instead of after I reveal the location of my domicile. Looking all around, there was no evidence that I had been spotted.

I silently moved the trash from my entrance and slid inside the concrete block building. I left one lantern on when I left, and its light was sufficient to illuminate most of the store's sales room. I turned on another and walked all the aisles and back rooms just to make sure I was still alone. No visitors, thank goodness. I can block the exit again and settle in for the night. I had set out a pack of peanuts and a string cheese that looked unspoiled. If that wouldn't satisfy my stomach, I could snap into a beef jerky. Those things had been hurting my stomach lately though. The next day I would need to find some more real food. Maybe wander back to the houses in the woods to the east. It would be a half a mile at least to go that far back, but it would be worth it if I could score real nutritious consumables.

As I began working on barricading the store entrance I heard talking outside. I dove for cover behind the door frame and waited. It sounded like the two women from earlier, the ones with the sword. Did they follow me?

"We know you are in there," one of them said calmly. "Don't be scared. We just want to talk. Maybe do some trading."

I didn't buy it. They had weapons and carried themselves like they took whatever they wanted. I wouldn't expect a fair trade if any. And what did they have to trade? Neither of them even had a backpack or handbag when I saw them earlier.

"Come on now, boy," the same woman said. "We ain't leaving until you acknowledge us at least. It's polite to hear offers before you decline a chance at trading. We might have exactly what you are looking for."

"What do we have that he wants?" the other woman asked, seemingly a little less intelligent than her partner.

"Well, you could give him some pussy like you did with that other guy..."

"Fuck you!" the dumber female shouted. "Why don't you fuck him this time?"

"Okay, okay," the first one replied. "Nobody needs to get fucked unless there be willing parties involved. I was just thinking that one guy on his own might be missing female companionship. It could be our best offer in his eyes. I don't know. What do you want to offer in trade?"

"Nothing!" she answered. "We just take what we want. We got the weapons. I didn't see none on him."

"Damn, Cheryl! He can fucking hear us, you know. I swear, you are dumb as shit sometimes. I don't believe you really are my sister. Mom must have slept around with retards before you were born."

Though the conversation was humorous, I had to think of ways to get out of this mess. Could I prevent them from breaking into the building? Should I exit and try to make peace? Was I desperate enough to consider either one of them attractive? Truth was, I didn't get that good of a look at them before. But that kind of thinking was going to get me killed.

I figured I could take them both in hand to hand combat, but they each had golf clubs and one had a sword. All I had was a baseball bat beside the door that I found behind the register. There was a handgun back there too, but no bullets anywhere to be found. I guess I could bluff. Or, would that make it worse? I'd be exposed with no ammo if they didn't feel like backing down.

As I considered these things carefully, I heard noise at the back door. I peeked out the doorway quickly to see if one of the two women had gone around back. Nope, they were both still standing there arguing. The stupider sister was a little heavy for my taste. She was the one with the sword. The other one had long wavy hair and didn't look too bad. Both were wearing jean shorts and dirty tank tops exposing dark tattoos on random body parts. Stop, I told myself. Now was not the time to start checking out the girls.

So, neither of them went to the back door. The noise continued. It was obvious that someone was prying away my barricade to get in. They must have another member to their gang. Then, I overheard more of the conversation out front.

"He ain't coming out," chubby said. "Are we just going to wait here while Earl kills him inside?"

Ah, they had a man in their group. He would no doubt be the leader. Maybe I should focus on defeating him first. At this point, I knew nothing about him though. Was he bigger than me? Did he have a weapon? Was he stupid, or would I have a hard time outsmarting him?

Just then the last barrier in the back room crashed to the floor. I knew the guy was inside now. I didn't have to wait long before he entered the sales room with a complete lack of caution. If I did have a gun, he would be dead before he knew it. So, he wasn't too bright then. What he did have was a small caliber rifle. Without even bothering to take aim he fired a round in my direction. I heard the pop of the bullet and the splintering of the wooden door frame behind me. I quickly decided the democratic approach would be a poor choice with this guy. I bolted out the front door before he could fire another shot.

The two women took up haphazard battle stances with weapons raised, standing maybe ten feet directly in front of the store entrance. The shiny blade of the sword was most definitely intimidating. I wouldn't want to be hit in the head with the golf club the other was holding either. It looked to maybe be a seven iron, as if that mattered. I bolted directly for the heavier girl figuring this was my opportunity for surprise. Indeed, they both looked shocked, screaming out as they swung their weapons in my direction like I was a bumble bee that took them unawares at a picnic. That was when I realized that I forgot to bring the baseball bat. The smarter girls club missed me by a good two feet since I wasn't headed in her direction. The dumber one's sword was headed for the top of my head. It managed to only contact some hair as my shoulder slammed into her hips, throwing her off her feet awkwardly. She landed on her ass as the weapon slipped from her hand. Her head then hit the asphalt with a crack.

I didn't have time to wait and see if she was okay. Her sister swung the club again from behind me. I thought for sure it would take me in the shoulder. I braced for contact and held out my hand to deflect the blow as much as I could. It barely grazed my fingertips, causing them to sting something terrible. But I couldn't really feel it right away. When she swung it again, I grabbed it with my left hand prior to it gaining any momentum. Before she could let go of it, I yanked hard causing her to stumble toward me. I grabbed her other wrist with my right hand and swung her around until my right arm had her in a loose choke hold.

"Hey!" the guy yelled as he finally exited the store. He was big. Both muscular and fat. Well, he had a big belly anyway. This guy was dark skinned and wore only camo cargo shorts and tan suede boots. His muscles bulged much more than mine. I immediately decided not to put myself in a position where he could pin me down. I quickly shuffled around to place the girl between me and the gun. "What happened to Cheryl?" he asked.

"He killed her," the girl I held coughed out. "I think she's dead. She ain't moving." When she started sobbing against my chest it cut me straight to my heart. I didn't want to kill anyone. I hoped the girl would recover. I looked over and her sister was right. The chubby one wasn't moving. She wasn't resting comfortably either. Her mouth was wide open, and one leg looked twisted awkwardly. I tried to tell myself that she would be okay, but it didn't look good.

"Let Tammy go or I'll shoot ya!" the guy barked out.

"I think you'll shoot me if I do let her go," I replied as calmly as I could muster.

"Hell, I don't give a shit about Tammy," he said. "I'll shoot right through her to kill your sorry ass."

"Hey!" Tammy took exception to the remark.

"He won't shoot her," a female voice said from somewhere over by the parked cars near the street. The lot was rough black top with no lines for parking spots. Three vehicles sat by the curb at Hollywood Avenue, and two others were sitting at random angles closer to the highway. There were no street lights, of course, but the moon in the clear sky illuminated the area enough. "He loves her." We all looked over, but I couldn't see anyone there.

"You love me, Earl?" Tammy asked.

"What? No! I mean, this is not the time to discuss it. Damn it, Tammy. I'm trying to get you out of the way.

Hey, boy! Who is that over by the cars? Tell her to come over here now or I'll shoot you where you stand."

"No, he won't," the voice said again. It sounded like a young woman, and maybe a little frightened. I was surprised that anyone would get involved in somebody else's mess. I had no idea who the person could be. I was certain that we had never met. Well, at least not in the last few weeks since the world completely went to shit. "He won't take a chance on hitting Tammy by accident," she declared from her hiding spot.

Earl then swung his rifle to aim in the general direction of the parked cars and fired off a shot that hit something metal. The hidden girl let out a startled squeak. When Earl looked ready to fire again, I took my chance. I threw Tammy to the ground hard enough to keep her from coming after me in the next few seconds. Then, I bolted toward the rifle bearer with adrenaline speed.

Instead of sending another bullet toward my concealed friend he quickly refocused on me and squeezed the trigger. Though charging at him as fast as I could, I could clearly see straight down the barrel of the rifle. His aim was true. Time slowed way down as I came to realize that I was about to be shot. My guess was that it would strike me in the neck or chest. Nowhere near as fast as a bullet, obviously, I still tried to dodge the shot. I grunted as I raised my hand instinctively in the path of the projectile.

My head and arms struck the man in the knees after the rifle round buzzed past my shoulder, barely catching my shirt threads. He had missed somehow. I felt Earl's fat belly and elbows strike my back as his legs flew backwards causing him to land on top of me on the ground. We both grunted loudly with the impact as Tammy started screaming profanity somewhere behind me. Then Earl rolled off and puked on the ground. I quickly scrambled to grab the rifle before either of them could realize what was happening.

I stood there and waited as comprehension appeared on Tammy's face and Earl wiped his puke from his chin.

"Hold on now," he said with a rougher voice than before. Drops of spittle the color of whatever he had eaten last flew in all directions as he spoke. "We weren't really going to shoot you."

"No?" I replied, unable to hold back my laughter. I knew that I had not imagined the gunshots. I could tell that Earl came to realize that he would not be able to talk his way out of this. He was completely at my mercy. "I tell you what. Why don't you both head on down New Hampshire Avenue towards DC with your hands in the air. No, scratch that. Grab Chreyl's fat ass and carry her all the way to the city. If I ever see you again, I will kill you without a word. Got it?"

Tammy looked very angry, then turned her attention to her sister crawling on the ground. Cheryl had woken up but was unable to stand on her own. Despite the attack on my life, I was glad to see that I hadn't caused her death. Surprisingly, Earl had a tear in his eye as he mouthed the words, "thank you." He was clearly disappointed in the way things worked out, and ready to concede. I watched as they gathered their wounded friend and dragged her down the street. Tammy tried to yell threats back at me, but Earl kept shutting her up. Eventually, their three forms faded into the darkness on the highway.

It wasn't until I was sure that they were gone that I turned my attention to the parked cars. Lowering the rifle to face the ground I called out. "Hey over there. Thanks for your help. Are you okay?"

I waited for a response, but none came. Just before I opened my mouth to speak again, I noticed slow, cautious movement behind the pickup truck. A girl's head gradually raised up into view as she began walking around the vehicle. She looked at the rifle.

"I'm not going to shoot you," I said. "Why would I? You just helped me. Possibly even saved my life." I gently placed the gun on the ground beside me to reinforce my good intentions. It must have helped because she walked less cautiously toward me until I could see her well in the moonlight. She was utterly beautiful.

CHAPTER TWO:

The girl that had just helped me defeat three enemies, or at least distracted them enough so I could do so, stood silently before me. If I had to guess I would say that she was about five foot, four inches, and maybe a hundred and twenty pounds. She was small breasted and had just enough muscle tone to suggest that she worked out with five-pound weights and lived in a fourth-floor apartment. I surmised that she was probably about my age and had silky long straight blond hair. The moonlight further revealed piercing blue eyes and fair skin.

She was dressed light and casual like myself. The increased temperatures since the comet struck Asia months ago had everyone skimpily garbed. Her short blue shorts and bulky blue sneakers showed off her sexy slender legs. A white t-shirt with a small Maryland Terrapin logo above the left breast covered her modest chest with about two inches of flat belly exposed. Her round face looked flawless in the dim light. Those large blue eyes had me thinking that she might be an anime model of my own hallucination.

I tried to speak, but my words were caught in my throat as my heart pounded against my chest. I was never confident when speaking to girls in general. Beautiful women like the perfect piece of DNA standing before me pretty much crippled me. Finally, I was able to say, "Hey."

"Hey," she replied softly.

I saw her check me out as well, and I began to wonder how she would judge me by my orange, quick-dry cargo shorts and black acrylic t-shirt. I did my best to keep my clothes as clean as possible in this dirty, burnt down new world. My black basketball shoes were a little scuffed up, but in good shape for the most part. When she looked me in the eyes again, I just couldn't speak.

Finally, she said, "I'm Alexa."

"Mason," I choked out. I must have been holding my breath. "My name is Mason."

A few more seconds passed as I stood there in stage fright. Eventually, she showed signs of annoyance and shrugged. I began to fear that she might turn and leave. I couldn't let that happen.

"I'm sorry," I said as I lowered my gaze to the ground. It was easier to speak if I wasn't looking directly at her. "I get a little shy sometimes around pretty... I mean, I don't get to talk to people much these days. Sorry, again. It's nice to meet you Alexa."

"You, too, Mason," she answered serenely. "It's okay."

"Thanks," I replied. I was not sure if I was thanking her for not being put off by my shyness, or her willingness to talk to me a little more. I believed that I wasn't a bad looking guy. However, I had never really acquired a girlfriend and my lack of confidence around the ladies was very embarrassing.

"Well, hey," I said alternating glances between her attractiveness and the asphalt. "Thanks for your help. I know you don't know me, but you are welcome to join me inside, if you want. I mean, it's generally not safe to stand around out in the open like this."

She nodded, "I agree. We can go inside if you don't mind."

"Okay, great," I responded. "I don't mind at all. Is it okay if I pick up the rifle?"

"Sure," Alexa answered as she began to step toward me and in the direction of the building. "Let's get inside and we'll talk some more."

The entrance was clear, and I figured I better leave it that way for now. I didn't want this hot young lady to feel like I was trapping her in. But, before it got too late, I knew I would have to barricade both the front and back doors for safety. Would she be interested in staying the night? I don't mean like sleeping with me, of course. But this was a fairly secure place to stay. Maybe she needed somewhere to sleep. Would she trust me enough to do that?

As I entered the store, I realized that the place was not up to standards for receiving guests. Until now, I had only thought about making it safe and comfortable. If this were the old world, and I was bringing a pretty girl home, she would bolt by now. Though not as shitty as the area around us, it was still a mess.

"I'm sorry," I muttered embarrassingly. "The place isn't as nice as it..."

"It's fine," she said softly, much closer behind me then I realized. My breath caught again as I thought about having a beautiful young lady following me into my makeshift home. I was so nervous. I had been bent on survival for so long. I didn't think my old shyness would debilitate me like this.

Once we reached the sales-counter I realized that I didn't have any chairs set out for guests. I was about to apologize again when she stopped me. We were standing there in the dim light of the lantern close enough to reach out and touch each other.

"Mason," she said. "It's okay. Don't worry about the place, and don't worry about whether I will trust you. Honestly, I've kind of been watching you for a couple days. And, I feel like I have a good read on you."

"You've been watching me?" I asked, surprised. I had not seen her around, that was for sure. Was she super stealthy or was my recon slipping? I immediately began retracing my steps to remember if I had done anything lately that I would be ashamed of. Then I realized that I had not said much yet. How did she know what I was thinking?

"Uh, not to be impolite, but how did you know what I was about to say? I mean, that I was going to apologize again. And, to think of it, how did you know that Earl loved Tammy and wouldn't shoot her?"

Alexa shrugged. I could see that she was struggling with whether to say something or not. I tried my best to hold my stare waiting for a reply, getting slowly more comfortable with her presence. Eventually, she did answer.

"I just have a talent for reading people."

"Is it like mind reading?" I asked. Again, quickly embarrassed about my thoughts since meeting her. Could she tell that I was so strongly attracted to her? Just a moment ago I thought about how nice it would be to place my arm around that slender waist of hers. Did she know what I was thinking?

"No," she replied quickly. "I can't read minds. It's just a feeling that I get. It's more like intuition."

"Oh, okay," I said. "So, you can't tell what I'm thinking right now?"

"No," she answered timidly while biting her lip. "I can only tell that you are shy and polite, and that you think I'm pretty. But you don't need intuition to figure that out. Your awkwardness, if you'll forgive me, is obvious. I can add that I get the feeling that you are a good person. That combined with your skill in fighting off intruders has me wondering if you are interested in a roommate. I hope that I'm not out of line in asking. I know you just met me, but I've gotten to know you a little bit already. Sorry for not introducing myself earlier."

"No," I answered quickly. "That's fine. It's a dangerous world out there. You have to be cautious. I completely understand. And, yes, you are definitely welcome to stay if you want."

"I don't eat much," she said. "And I can do some cooking and cleaning. Beyond that, I'm probably not worth a lot. I can't fight at all."

"Actually, your intuition in itself is probably worth your room and board. And, as you already know, I wouldn't mind the company."

"Excellent," she said, smiling for the first time. She was even more beautiful than before. "Should I help you barricade the doors?"

"Oh! Yes. I mean, no, I can do it. I meant yes, it needs to be done." She watched as I stacked the usual stuff in front of the store entrance, then began touring the place as I sealed up the back. I gathered a little extra food and pulled two chairs out of the back office so we could eat behind the sales counter. That was the area where I kept most of my supplies. I split my bedding into two so she could sleep comfortably at the other end of the narrow space. I was delighted to see that she was pleased with the arrangement.

It was too early to sleep for me, and I was excited to learn more about my new guest. Alexa told me that she was twenty-one years old, just two years older than me, and a student at the University of Maryland. I was right about the fourth-floor apartment, seeing those toned calves. She lived in a dorm in College Park until things got too bad to stay. She was originally from Hagerstown Maryland, but there was no reason to return there since her parents already passed away. She had some friends at college that she was traveling with, but they all eventually died from the viruses. It turned out that she was the only one totally immune in her group.

I was surprised to learn that the gift of extra intuition was a recent development for her. She said that she began sensing additional things about people just a couple weeks ago. I got the feeling that she had seen more of the world since the catastrophe than I had, so I focused on learning about what was going on out there. She was able to confirm that the vast majority of survivors were female. She laughed pretty hard when I told her that I called the sub human people skunks and skanks. Evidently most people thought they were zombies. She guessed that there were at least three times as many of those decaying creatures than regular survivors. The majority of humans died from the multi-pandemic. Those that lived but didn't deteriorate appeared to be completely immune. There were several viruses that attacked humanity. That's why it took months to kill off an estimated nine hundred and ninety-nine out of every thousand.

In this new era of self-preservation and distrust I was very much surprised to see how quickly Alexa became comfortable with my presence. It wasn't long before she dosed off, curled up in the pile of blankets on the floor. Too hot for covering up, her sexy slender form remained exposed. If it were some other lonely guy here with her, she would be taking a serious risk. I, however, had always been a gentleman. It was how I was raised.

Though the battle I had just survived may have been my most traumatic, I believed it ended up being a very good day. I began to fantasize about how much more hopeful the future could be with Alexa as a roommate. Not only was she very attractive, her friendly personality would make her a joy to be around after all these solitary days and nights. The fact that she trusted me so easily broke down all the usual barriers of first contact these days. I would need to do a better job of keeping her alive than I had done with others in the past. Her willingness to depend on me could make all the difference in that respect.

I knew that I should be more cautious than this. I basically invited in a stranger to stay the night. I was letting her appearance sway me too easily. Eventually I fell asleep in my usual spot which was about ten feet from sleeping beauty. I was positioned closer to the door with a protection mentality. If someone were able to sneak in past the barricades, they would get to me first. I had become an extremely light sleeper lately, though. The chances of being approached while sleeping was slim to none.

In the morning I woke to the sound of her sneakers softly squeaking as she walked around the counter into the main room of the store. I remained quiet, raising to one knee so I could watch her unaware. This was my opportunity to see if she had any mischievous ideas when she offered to join me here. So far, she was just wandering the aisles checking out what merchandise was left on the shelves. Nearly half of the beer and wine were untouched. I cleaned up much of the mess of broken bottles shortly after I moved in, but I could now see clearly that it was a superficial job. But Alexa wasn't paying much attention to my housekeeping skills. Eventually she grabbed a bottle of red wine and started walking back to the counter. I tried to duck down before she could see me.

"I don't know what we have planned for dinner today," she spoke just loud enough to make it clear that she knew I was awake. "But I think this bottle of Cabernet will probably go well with it."

I nearly laughed. It was the first thing I really found funny in quite some time. I stayed quiet. It was almost like a game. I was very excited to hear her making dinner plans with me, but I felt like I should pretend to still be sleeping. I guess I didn't want to be caught peeping on her. I laid back down on my pillow before she came in view around the corner.

"Sorry, Mason," she said plainly. "I could sense that you were awake. Do you drink wine?"

I gave up the facade and sat up to face her. I don't know if she had brushed her hair since waking, but she stilled looked perfect in the lantern light. I figured once we got outside in the daylight, she would have to have some physical flaws that would dent my fascination with her. Perhaps skin blemishes. Maybe a dumpy ass, or a poorly placed mole. I almost hoped that she had several flaws.

"Uh, yes. Sometimes. I suppose that I drank beer more than wine before the, you know."

"I'm guessing the beer is not as good warm," she said, sitting down crosslegged to look at me as we talked. She must have a razor in her backpack because her legs were recently shaved. "Hanging out in a beer and wine store must have you drunk half the time. Did you consume all those missing bottles?" She cracked a playful smile.

"No," I answered smiling. "The store had been looted quite a bit before I got here. I do admit that I tried some of the craft beer, out of curiosity. And I think you are right. It's not so good warm. I did have a bottle of Moscato that tasted like candy. That was probably the only day that I got drunk."

"Ah, Moscato," she said. "So, what are our plans for today?"

"Well, I was thinking we could go looking for better food. I had already intended to do that. Now, with you here, I feel like it's a must. I'm kind of embarrassed that I don't have a better set up for you."

"I know," she replied sincerely. "But, it's okay. Honestly, this is so much better than what I've been dealing with for weeks. Maybe together we can focus on improvements. Is it okay if I start working on tidying up a bit?"

"Sure," I responded. "Did you want something to eat first?"

"I'm okay for now. What I could really use is a cup of coffee. Maybe we should raid an old Starbucks. You think?"

"I actually have some coffee," I replied proudly. I had rigged up a system where I could use a small flame to brew coffee. The beer store had cases of brew packets in the back, and a couple decanters. It didn't taste fantastic, but the hot morning beverage was a luxury these days. I would gladly brew some for my new friend. In fact, I would do almost anything to keep her around.

"Oh my God!" Alexa exclaimed with more enthusiasm than I expected. She stood up abruptly in her excitement. "You are my hero already. Show me how you make it. I can have coffee ready for us every morning."

I gathered the supplies and showed her the process that I had been using to brew coffee. We discussed some possible adjustments that could be made. I was standing just inches from her incredibly sexy body much of the time. I tried my best to control myself, but I couldn't help checking out the form of her small breasts below her t-shirt. Her skimpy black bra was clearly visible through the white fabric and appeared to be more like a bikini top. The couple inches of exposed soft skin on her lower back was clear of ink. To me, that was a good sign.

Up close, her face was surprisingly beautiful. Especially those oversized bright blue eyes. She had me mesmerized briefly each time she looked at me. A tiny pointed chin completed the round face to give that anime goddess appearance. In the dim light there appeared to be blue streaks around her temples, and more just below her neck. Was it make-up, or dirt, or my imagination?

"What are you?" she asked. "Twelve years old? You're like a little school boy around me."

"I'm sorry, Alexa," I replied bashfully as I took a step back.

"Honestly," she said without turning to face me. "I'm flattered. But it is a bit too much. This extra perception that I now have is an overload."

"I understand," I responded quietly. "I'll give you more space until I get accustomed to having you around. Please don't let this scare you off. I assure you that you don't need to be scared of me."

"I believe you, Mason. But I'm still learning about this extra intuition thing. I really have too little experience with it to know if it is accurate. It could just be wishful thinking on my part. So far, though, it hasn't let me down."

The rest of the morning we found projects to do that kept us separated most of the time. Alexa worked up a shopping list for our afternoon supply run as we both made great progress in improving the condition of our habitat. I fortified the back door to prevent another Earl type from barging in. By the time we were ready for lunch I felt myself behaving much more calmly around my new roommate. I avoided looking at her more than needed. I'm sure that helped. Unfortunately, I still felt like she required some distance. I vowed to myself to be patient. It was extremely unlikely, I thought, that another beautiful young woman would want to move in with me. I had to make this work.

CHAPTER THREE:

I started peeling away the layers of various debris blocking the old store entrance. We were all prepared for our first foraging mission together. The plan was to gradually head east, selecting a few suitable residences to raid for supplies. I really wanted to get to some of the bigger homes that were way back in the woods. They may have been protected by alarms long enough to ward off intruders. Perhaps one of them would have exactly what we need.

"Wait," Alexa said softly. I stopped moving the bulky barrier pieces and listened for what she might have heard. She was staring blankly at the entrance.

"Did you hear something?"

"No," she whispered. "I'm just reaching out with my gift to see if I can sense anyone out there before we go barging out." That's when I saw the unusual blue streaks return to her face and chest. They were exquisitely coordinated with her eye color and resembled masquerade makeup.

"Are you aware," I said quietly, "that you have some blue coloring that comes and goes on your skin? Does that only happen when you are using your gift?"

"I think so," Alexa answered. "Did you know that the veins on your arms and legs glow orange when you are fighting?"

"Bullshit!" I answered without thinking. I wasn't actually calling her a liar, but I thought she must be joking. Orange veins? My body? My favorite color?

Alexa stopped staring forward and turned to me. "No, really. They kind of pulsed orange while you were fighting those three assholes last night. I think that you have an extraordinary power of your own. I would guess that it is your ability to dodge swords and bullets. I honestly don't know you survived. I thought for sure I was going to lose you before we even met."

"You may be right," I answered, considering it seriously. I remember being amazed during the fight that everything was missing me. Maybe Earl realized it, too. That's why he conceded so quickly. Well, that and me taking his gun. I looked down at my arms, but there was nothing to see at the moment, of course.

"We'll have to test it later today," she said with a playful smile. "I can throw dangerous shit at you and you can dodge them all."

"Why does it have to be dangerous shit? Can't you throw pillows first?"

"Maybe it has to be something that will kill you for your power to be activated. I don't know. We can start with safer stuff if you are scared that I might hurt you. I saw some beer pong balls at the counter."

"That sounds like a better idea to me," I replied unoffended. "When do we test your superpower?"

"We've been testing it all along. Just now when I mentioned throwing dangerous shit at you, I felt a mild trepidation for a second. Am I right?"

"Maybe," I answered. "So, is there anybody outside we need to worry about before we exit?"

She shook her pretty head and said, "Not as far as I can tell. But I'll keep my senses sharp as we go. Are the blue sections of my skin ugly?"

"Alexa, nothing about you is remotely ugly. "

Her sincere smile let me know that the compliment was appreciated, and that maybe I had made progress in keeping my emotions under control. Just to be safe, I continued to avert my eyes as much as I could.

We proceeded down Hollywood Avenue patiently dodging from one house to another and staying off the street. These small buildings had undoubtedly belonged to middle income families. That meant that they were more easily raided and probably had less worth taking. We skipped most of them completely as we started zigzagging through the crumbling neighborhood. Fires had apparently swept through every area that I had seen lately, causing many of the places to be unfit for entry.

The sun was high in the sky by the time we reached a dwelling that I thought would be worth our time. The front of the home was an elaborate combination of fancy wood and stone with large windows cut at steep angles toward the roof. The main entry was closed and to the right was a three-car garage that appeared to be secure.

There was no debris in the front yard or any busted windows. I believed this could be the jackpot if we could find a way inside. It was highly unlikely that an alarm was still powered. I motioned for my new partner to join me around back. We'd be much less noticeable trying to open a back door.

Together we admired the plentiful bird feeders and wind chimes as we moved deliberately through the tall grass. Alexa looked moderately comfortable at my side and glanced my way when I briefly considered holding her hand. Maybe one day she would be my girlfriend, if I could ever get past that emotion tracker of hers. Perhaps a relationship with someone that acquired that gift would be much more difficult than normal. Based on her alluring appearance and delightful personality I considered it would be well worth it.

We both cleared the corner of the large elegant house at the same time and stopped abruptly in our tracks. The gut-wrenching smell carried by the mild breeze hit us at the same time as the shocking sight. Three stray dogs were about halfway through devouring two dead skanks. When Alexa gagged uncontrollably all three beasts turned in our direction and growled.

"Shit!" I exclaimed, raising my baseball bat instinctively. Would it be enough to hold them off? It was the only weapon that I had, and Alexa was completely unarmed. I hadn't thought to bring my recently acquired rifle. It turned out to only have a couple bullets left anyway. In the anxious moment that followed I could see that one dog was a black and white Collie with the fierce teeth of a wolf. Had it mutated? The Doberman looked normal, though still very much intimidating. The other was a German Shepherd with oversized claws and fangs. It had definitely been altered by the viruses, I surmised. I had seen mutant animals roaming the area before, but never came face to face with any until now.

When the Doberman returned to noisily eating the rotten corpse closest to it, I thought we might get lucky. Grievously, the ferocious Collie advanced and the German Shepherd followed its lead. We backed away slowly hoping that our body language would be correctly interpreted as an apology for interrupting their meal. Regrettably, it was not. They continued to steadily gain ground as we retreated. I knew that we couldn't easily outrun them. We would have to pick our best spot for a fight.

There was an alcove section of the house where we could at least avoid being surrounded. I backed us in there and readied my weapon. A rusty drainpipe painted the same dark brown as the wood siding stealthily climbed the corner of the alcove. It rose to a slight pitched roof that was maybe just eight feet off the ground. If Alexa could get herself up there, she would probably be out of reach of the crazed animals.

"Get behind me," I said as calmly as I could, applying the palm of my hand to her flat belly. "Try to climb the drainpipe." I thought she might object to attempting the physical feat due to her slight stature. But, the fear in her eyes indicated that she was ready to do whatever it took to flee these predators. Her sudden movement drew in the Collie first. Before it could reach the lovely girl, I struck it hard in the shoulder with the wooden bat. It let out the desired and satisfying yelp as the blow sent it falling away from the house. At least the mutation didn't make them super strong.

Before I could swing the bat back into position to defend my friend, the German Shepherd successfully clawed Alexa's delicate ankle while she was halfway up the brown pipe. She screamed, of course, but did not fall. My next swing took the attacking beast in the back of the head with all the force I could muster. It immediately fell limp to the ground. The collie then looked at the motionless animal, then back to me. I couldn't immediately tell if it was angry at me for killing its friend, or more scared of me for what I had just done. Then the ferocious animal surprised me by jumping on the unresponsive dog and ripping it's flesh open with its own jaws.

Thankfully, Alexa had made it to the roof by then and frantically called for me to join her. I waited to make sure I wouldn't be attacked when I turned away, then followed her in a veiled panic. We cautiously backed away from the edge until we encountered a closed bedroom window. I used a fallen branch laying on the roof to break the plane of glass and clear the dangerous shards for safe entry. Soon we found ourselves inside a large bedroom with bulky furniture. Together we pushed the heavy chest of drawers in front of our entry point to prevent the dogs from possibly coming after us. It wasn't until then that we felt safe enough to check Alexa's leg. The animal's enlarged claws had scratched her pretty good, but it wasn't bleeding too terribly bad.

"Does it hurt?" I asked, like a fool.

"Yes, it hurts!"

"Sorry. Here let me get it cleaned up." I found a bathroom adjacent and soaked the green hand towel I found there to clean her wound. I didn't even realize at first that I had placed my hand on the back of her lower left leg to raise up the ankle for cleaning. I was actually touching the girl of my dreams. She didn't object, so I continued to care for her injury and wrapped it tightly with a flex bandage from the medicine cabinet.

"Thank you," she said with tears in her eyes.

"I'm sorry that I didn't get that dog before he could do this to you."

"I know," she responded. "It's not your fault. I think you did a great job of getting us out there alive. We're lucky I didn't get hurt worse. I'm sorry that I'm not much help in a fight."

"No, that's okay," I replied. "I guess your extra sense didn't pick up on the animals."

"No, I had no idea that there was anything in the back yard. I would have sensed the zombies if they were still alive, I think."

"They are not actually zombies," I replied. "Zombies are undead or walking dead. These extremely sick people are still alive. That's why they stink so bad. Even a human corpse doesn't smell as bad as these things."

"Okay," she submitted. "Skanks then. I can usually pick up their hunger and desperation, but it's less powerful than normal people."

Again, without really thinking about it, I picked Alexa up off the floor and placed her on the bed. I did so by putting one arm under her arms then the other below her legs. She didn't weigh much, but I didn't think that I could carry her all the way home. I waited a couple minutes for her to relax before deciding what to do next.

"Maybe you should rest here while I check the house for supplies," I suggested.

"Please don't leave me, Mason," she pleaded softly.

"I won't leave you, Alexa. Don't worry about that. Can you walk enough to join me?"

"I think so," she said, sliding to the side of the bed and raising one arm toward me for help. I placed my right arm around her slender frame to help her up. The injury was more painful than debilitating. By the time we left the bedroom she was capable of walking while leaning against the wall. That freed up my hands for collecting supplies and facing any obstacles that we might encounter. I grabbed a bunch of medical supplies from the bathroom and tossed them in her backpack.

The home looked like it had never been ransacked, just like I had hoped. We gathered lots of canned and boxed food as well as two gallons of bottled water. There ended up being enough good stuff that we decided to take a child's red wagon from the garage. We might even come back another time for the rest. I told Alexa to ride on top of the wagon full of stuff, but she insisted on walking instead. That was okay with me because it gave me the opportunity to have my arm around her much of the time. It wasn't long before I was comfortable being that close to her without getting overly excited. Even with the bandage and the limp she was gorgeous. Maybe even more so, in a damsel in distress kind of way.

The dogs were still working on their disgusting meals, so we left through the front door and locked it behind us. Again, we moved cautiously through the neighborhood on our way back to the beer and wine store that was becoming our home. We spotted a few deer along the way, some cats and dogs, and a handful of skanks. But none ever spotted us or considered us worth their attention. We happily made it all the way back to the store without another incident.

After moving the layered barricade from the entrance, I turned to help Alexa get safely inside. She totally surprised me by hugging me instead.

"Thank you, Mason," she said in my ear.

"For what?" I asked as I returned the hug with calculated restraint, placing my arms around her lower back. My muscles seemed a little bigger each week, despite a lack of disciplined exercise. I didn't want to cause her discomfort.

"For not leaving me. I'm sorry for giving you a hard time about your feelings before. It was not fair of me."

"Don't worry about it," I said. "Let's get inside and have something to eat. Aren't you hungry?"

"Oh, yes," Alexa answered as she released the embrace. "I'm starving."

We spent the rest of the day organizing our supplies and cooking two enjoyable meals. I cleaned Alexa's wound a couple more times and was happy to see that it was beginning to heal. She no longer needed my assistance in walking, and the retained limp was minimal. I found some pain medicine for her, but she was hesitant to take it worrying that it would make her drowsy. She said that she had not taken any kind of medicine since she was a child. I found that unusual, but everyone was untitled to their own views on health. I read somewhere that those with the naturalistic approach lived longer anyway.

We were much more optimistic than before about our water supplies and decided to wash up a bit before our second meal of the day. I changed into my black sport shorts and orange stretch workout tee, plus clean socks. I tried the body spray I snatched from the house and figured its scent was much more appealing than my sweaty self. Alexa switched to her other pair of short shorts. These were black cotton and left most of her sexy thighs exposed. The light green ribbed tank top hugged her slender form nicely and was cut low enough to reveal a good amount of her modest breasts. Her fragrance was the same as when we met, so she must have a perfume in her bag. When she walked in with her new outfit, I felt a surge of testosterone run through me again. She briefly gave me a concerned look as the blue streaks flashed on her skin.

"I'm sorry," I apologized quickly, turning away. "You look very nice."

"Thank you," she replied genuinely. "I think I'm getting more used to your attention, Mason. You have been every bit a gentleman to me since I arrived. It's not fair of me to judge you by these feelings that I am sensing. Can I ask you about what you are feeling when you look at me? I think it could help us to talk about it. Do you mind?"

"Uh, I'm not sure."

"Well, when I feel in spike in your attraction to me it's like a warning buzzer going off in my head. As I said, you have done nothing to warrant my distrust, so I would like to better understand what you are feeling in that moment. That way when it happens, I actually know what is going on."

"It's embarrassing, Alexa," I said shyly, turning away. "It's not fair that you can pick up on my emotions and I don't get to know what you are thinking or feeling."

"Okay," she answered. "I understand. Well, I'm not a real open person about my feelings either. Let me just say that I like you a lot. You are very kind and protective. I also think you are a good-looking man. How is that?"

"It helps," I smiled.

"So, I already know that you like me, too. And that you find me sexually attractive. Just tell me something about what you are thinking when I feel that surge from you. Are you wanting to have sex with me? Is it an uncontrollable urge?"

"No!" I responded immediately, turning to face her. The blue flashed around her temples again as her expression looked almost apologetic. "I mean, yes, being sexually attracted to you does mean that I'd like to, you know. But, it's not like I feel like attacking you. It's more like being touched emotionally by something very beautiful. Like a great piece of art, or an amazing waterfall. Please understand that I could never harm you or force myself on you."

"I believe you," she responded with a tear in her eye, smiling anyway. "Thank you for explaining it to me. Your compliment backed up by the genuine emotions I sense are probably the nicest thing anyone has ever said to me. I won't judge you wrong ever again, Mason. I promise. I truly appreciate you."

CHAPTER FOUR:

I awoke the next morning to the scent of fresh brewed coffee. Somehow, Alexa had gotten up before me without disrupting my sleep. Though having my new best friend prepare my favorite breakfast beverage was great, I was more than a little alarmed that I slept that sound. Waking easily was a critical requirement for survival in this dangerous new world.

Alexa's slender back was to me as she set an assortment of cookies from a package onto a paper plate, then poured two Styrofoam cups full of coffee. From experience, I knew that she already sensed that I was awake. As an experiment I decided to test her anyway. Hopefully, she would not be overly offended. Instead of focusing on her shapely thin calves or tight little butt, I visualized walking up behind her. Then wrapping my arms gently around her tapered waist and lightly pressing my lips against her bare shoulder.

Instantly, she tensed up as if a rat snuck up before her. Was this test a bad idea? Luckily, one second later she let out a slow smooth breath and said without turning around, "Good morning, Mason." It sounded like she was smiling, maybe even laughing. That was good.

"Good morning, Alexa." I was definitely smiling, thankful that my experiment went well. "Thanks for fixing coffee. How is your leg?"

Alexa carried the hot drinks and the dish of cookies around to set them on the counter before pulling back the bandage to show me her boo boo. "I think it's healing pretty good. I'm a little embarrassed that I cried like I did over it. I thought for sure it was cut up worse than it is. I appreciate you caring for it as well as you have. I think I can keep it clean from here on."

"Cool, cool," I replied, like an idiot, never knowing what to say. "What would you like to do today?"

"Well," she said, handing me a coffee and the plate of cookies. "You might think this is silly, but I was wondering if you would be interested in doing some redecorating?"

"Redecorating?"

"Actually, it would be mostly rearranging the main room here, and probably adding some furniture. I know we might not stay here forever, but I'd like for it to more closely resemble the rooms of a house while we are here. The office and storage rooms are too cramped, I think. The area behind the sales counter should work well for a kitchen. We would need a table and chairs for the dining room. The tough part would be acquiring a sofa for the living room. Then, we could move the shelving around to form walls. The nice thing about that would be that we could see over those walls in a defense scenario."

"So, you have been giving this a lot of thought," I said.

"Not really. It just kind of hit me this morning, then my mind starting racing with ideas."

"So," I asked timidly. "Are we playing house, Alexa?"

She crossed her arms as she looked at me, trying to figure out how serious the question was before responding, I think. "Mason, I'm not ready to commit to anything but roommates for now. You haven't given me any reason to want to leave. And, honestly, I would be surprised if you did anytime soon. You are a good survival partner, for sure. And, if you must know, I am starting to grow fond of having you around."

I nodded, not sure what to say. It was well known that I wanted her around.

"So, what do you think?" she asked.

"Let's do it."

We spent most of that morning moving the bulky wooden shelves around after removing all the alcohol first, of course. Areas where we felt the need for specific pieces of furniture, we marked the floor with some sidewalk chalk I had taken from a house weeks ago. I had no idea how we would safely transport a sofa and a dining room table. It seemed like moving into a house would be a better idea, if it were not for how this place was much easier to defend and already stocked with supplies.

Alexa worked up another shopping list for us. Women, always with shopping on their mind. We would try to get any large pieces of furniture from one of the houses that were very close to the store. We should be able to carry them that far, while keeping an eye out for danger. Other items, like fake plants, might take more effort to find. Despite the increased vulnerability needed to obtain some of these items, I was eager to get everything she wanted. If I could be the man that takes care of her, and make my place comfortable for her live in, I had my best chance of holding on to her. And that was very much my plan.

I figured that it was maybe mid-afternoon when we headed northeast to raid some more homes. I brought the wagon and several large plastic shopping bags. We could use them to carry supplies that we might stumble across as we searched for Alexa's comfort items. She grabbed so many throw pillows from the first house that I thought we should return to our place immediately. But Alexa said we could always leave half the pillows in another house if we find more valuable items. After three lengthy trips we had all the basics on our list except the sofa and managed to avoid any wandering predators. That's when I got an idea.

"Hey, Alexa? Do you think we could make do with a couple small church pews until we get the sofa? They'll be a lot easier to carry."

"Church pews?" she asked with obvious distaste for my idea. I felt a little stupid and uncaring after her response. Of course, she picked up on those emotions and adjusted her tone considerably. "Well, I'm not big on the idea long term, but if you prefer to do that for now, I can deal with it. We'll certainly need all those pillows and cushions then. Where is the closest church?"

I pointed at the steeple rising skyward in the next lot, casting its shadow over us. The church was directly behind the store on New Hampshire Avenue, facing the next street over. A chain link privacy fence with charred wooden slats stood between the two properties and the adjacent houses. We would have to go out to the main street to get there. The sizable building for worship was made of multi-shade brown brick and looked to have survived the fires quite well. However, I never checked out the inside while I was here since it seemed like a poor source for the survival items I needed. Pews, though, they should have plenty of those if the fires never made it inside. I just didn't want to carry a twenty-footer back the store. Something six to eight feet long would be great. If they were light enough, we might be able to tote two of the them together. I used to move benches in physical education class using that method all the time. It just required a helper.

We stowed all our acquired booty so far and sealed our makeshift home entrance back up before heading over to the neighborhood church. I insisted on using extra caution getting this close to the main highway. As we did our recon a few shuffling skanks meandered through the neighborhood on the other side. They probably wouldn't even notice us at this distance. Then a herd of about a dozen deer sprinted across the wide asphalt strip, chasing after a dog. Deer. Chasing a dog. Perhaps the animals had gone crazy from hunger or virus, or both. Anyway, it was the first time I had ever seen that for sure.

Eventually, I gave the okay to go around the fence. The tall grass on the other side had dried up so bad that it was crunchy beneath our footfalls. It was more annoying than anything else, still I made haste to get to the parking lot and beyond. A double glass door on the back of the building was in view. We headed there quickly only noticing on arrival that the glass was missing from one of the doors, and the frame was slightly bent up. Someone or something had already entered this building forcibly. That was clear.

Before I could lean against the battered doorway and listen for any activity, Alexa declared that she was sensing people inside.

"I can't tell for sure, but I believe that there is one normal person in there scared for their life. And, I sense a lot of hunger. There must be a bunch of the skanks attacking. Oh my God!" Alexa exclaimed as the emotions became overwhelming. "Mason, we have to help them!"

"Okay, okay," I answered quickly. The best decision, naturally, would be to not get involved. A bunch of skanks? Yeah, we should undoubtedly turn and go, forget about the pews. But Alexa's gift must have made her overly sympathetic to the people she was sensing. Except maybe in cases when she sensed them to be assholes.

"Alright, stay here and let me have a look."

I gingerly stepped across the carpeted hallway to peek into the spacious sanctuary beyond. The rotting flesh odor was getting undeniably stronger as I went. Then I could see that there were at least a dozen stinkies standing, and more scattered randomly on the floor. Some of them were obviously dead with busted heads and limbs. Their skin being ripped open released even more of the unbearable stench. I did my best not to gag, remembering how Alexa had drawn the attention of the wild dogs yesterday.

Huge stained-glass windows allowed in just enough light to see the whole open worship area. There were plenty of pews that appeared to be in good condition, even some smaller ones. The skanks and skunks, there were at least two males, were struggling to get around them as they all faced a common foe. At first, I didn't see their victim, as she was in a shadow. Her medium brown skin and darker clothing also provided some concealment. Her back was to me as well, and a pillar blocked some of my view, but she looked to be quite fit from what I could see.

One of the skunks that was hovering close finally dove at her. A spear rapidly shot out from the woman to pierce the attacker's exposed pale chest, before being pulled back in. The skunk let out a howl as dark red blood ran down his belly, and the skanks around him all responded in kind. The noise and scent combined desperately tried to convince my body to leave this nasty place. That's when I remembered I was supposed to be reporting back to Alexa about what was going on inside. I had left her out there alone, defenseless. When I turn toward the door, I was surprised to see her approaching me in the hallway. I pressed my finger to my lips encouraging her to be quiet. Then, I pulled her close so I could whisper in her ear.

"There are a dozen of them, at least. They are attacking a woman. The odds are not good, Alexa. Are you sure you want to get involved?"

"A woman?" she whispered back. That in itself should have not been alarming since the vast majority of survivors were female. Instead, I saw that she connected to the panic that she was feeling and associated it with someone weaker like herself. "We have to help her, don't we?"

For months I had been trying to adjust my mentality in my new surroundings. I had been raised to always help those in need. Even as a child I always held the door open for strangers and assisted my elderly relatives. In the early days of this world going to shit I still clung stubbornly to those values. Regrettably, it placed me and others in harm's way repeatedly. I vowed to toughen up and did my best to put my survival above that of any others. So far, I was not doing well with that endeavor. I too felt compelled to help the woman. I had a bat. She had a spear. Maybe together we could fight them off. But how would I protect Alexa during the battle?

Looking into the sanctuary again I saw the muscular black woman swing the spear at two skanks. They seemed to be trying to distract her as the chest bleeding skunk lunged again. I was expecting the battle to end then, making our decision for us. Instead, the woman swung a shiny hatchet down fiercely to split open the skunk's head. He fell to the ground without making another sound. The violent action not only shocked me it effectively caused every other stinky in the room to pause. I hoped that would be enough to scared them off, but the moment eventually passed, and they began to shuffle toward the warrior type woman again.

A plan began to form in my mind. The woman had two weapons, but she would be better off handing one of those weapons to a possible partner. Me. We could fight them off together, I believed. That way I could hand my bat to Alexa. Maybe that would keep her protected long enough for us to end this extremely unpleasant skirmish. When I handed the bat to my sexy friend, she already had her hand open to receive it. That made me question her abilities more, wandering if there was some mind reading going on after all. But now was not the time to focus on that. We needed to even up this battle fast.

I rushed into the large room yelling, "let me help!" Alexa was right on my heals but veered toward the area behind the woman as I had instructed. I wanted her protected during this unpredictable fight. The black woman turned to face us in a panic, obviously not registering us as helpers quick enough. Her agile body turned with precision as she whipped the small ax through the air in our direction. I felt my arms pulse with the ability that Alexa had claimed that I had, my veins likely turning orange. But the hatchet was not headed for me. It was somersaulting through the air toward my beautiful partner. Alexa's eyes got even bigger as she realized that she could not possibly dodge the weapon in time.

"NO!" I screamed, trying to alter my direction to block it from striking Alexa. I was nowhere near close enough to get in the weapon's path, though. Fortunately, both of us must have badly misjudged the projected course. The hatchet's blade struck the wooden wall about three feet away from its target with a thump. "Awesome!", I thought as I grabbed the handle and yanked it free. Alexa was still in shock, so I gently pushed her toward the safe area as I faced the numerous attackers. The woman turned the spear toward me, but I could see the beginning of relief in her eyes as she realized we were like her, full human.

"No," I said, raising my empty hand to her. "We're here to help." Surprisingly, all the decaying enemies just stood there. They watched the whole scene play out instead of taking advantage of the distraction. When the two of us formed a uniform front against them they began to doubt, looking at each other questioningly. Finally, the other skunk, the lone remaining male stepped forward. After a moment of studying us he turned to face the others without fully putting his back to us as he spoke.

"Go," he said, more clearly than any other skunk I've ever heard. "Done," he said then, sounding exhausted. When he turned to see the other male dead on the floor, he said sadly, "Gone." With that, they all slowly shuffled their stinky asses out the main door of the church, obviously not expecting us to chase after them. Looking around the floor, I saw five dead attackers, and two more crawling out miserably behind their comrades. There were no other regular people that I could see, so that woman had done a competent job of defending herself even before we arrived.

"Thanks," she said, apparently still hesitant to regard me as a friend. She glanced between my face and the hatchet in my hand. I could now see her more clearly. Though not as young as Alexa, she was also a very beautiful woman. Her creamy brown skin and brown eyes were alluring. The woman's curly hair was short and black, with red tips and streaks. The color matched her tight red t-shirt and sneakers. Skin tight black workout shorts completed the outfit and showed off her muscular build. She was visibly a fitness freak, but damn she looked sexy. Her bulging arms and legs tapered off to thin wrists and ankles. Her hands and feet were smallish, too. So, she was not big boned. Her intimidating appearance came from a lot of exercise.

I remembered my ability to dodge and considered it safe to return the weapon to her. It was also a calculated gesture of trust. I shifted the hatchet in my hand so that the handle faced her. She hesitated, then gladly accepted it.

"I'm Mason," I said. "And this is Alexa." My attractive blond companion slid over to stand closely beside me.

"Jada," the good looking, long faced woman said. Then she looked me up and down slowly. I couldn't tell if she was judging my ability to fight or thinking maybe I was sexy, too. Hell, she might think I'd make good eating. It was hard to the tell in this world. "My name is Jada," she said then more friendly. "It's nice to meet you, Mason. Thanks for your help."

I gestured to the corpses on the floor. "It looks like you were doing a pretty good on your own. You obviously have significant skill with those weapons."

"Thanks," she replied, finally taking a deep breath and beginning to relax. "I'm not sure I could have won the entire battle myself, though. At least not without injury. And, sorry for throwing the ax at your friend."

I turned to see if Alexa was going to respond. She didn't. In fact, she looked more than a little offended. I shrugged it off and was about to ask where the woman was staying. Maybe she needed a safe place and some friends, too. At the last second, I realized that was something that should be discussed with my roommate first.

"So," Jada asked. "Are you two a couple?"

Before I could respond Alexa slid her dainty hand in mine and said, "Yes." I wasn't sure if our relationship had indeed advanced to that point yet, or if she considered our new friend to be a threat to our bond. Either way, I was delighted. I squeezed her hand gently and nodded my agreement.

"Are you staying around here?" I asked, trying not to make it sound like a line I would use in a bar. "Or, are you just passing through?"

Jada hesitated once again, then answered carefully. "I've actually been staying here for a couple weeks. I mean, in one of the other rooms. Not here in the sanctuary. It's going to stink pretty damn bad in here for a while, but I should still be okay. I'll seal the doors between here and the other rooms, then let the beasts come in to eat these disgusting bodies. How about you two?"

"We have been staying in the beer store right behind the church." Alexa tensed up noticeably when I said it. Earlier she was all about saving this damsel in distress. Now, she acted like she wanted to keep her distance. It was confusing me. I decided to refrain from offering Jada to join us. It would be awesome to have two beautiful women as roommates, but not if it ruined my chances with Alexa. We talked for a couple more awkward minutes, then parted ways without meddling too much into each other's business. That had become the way of the world, lately. It was survival mode thinking.

"See you around neighbor," Jada said as we left through the way we had entered. It was obvious that she was consistently addressing me and barely acknowledging Alexa. I had seen women do that in movies before to understand what it meant.

"It was nice to meet you," Alexa responded in the most fake voice I had ever heard her use. Arm and arm we made our way stealthily back to the store, totally forgetting about wanting the pews. Once we were completely out of earshot, Alexa told me that she didn't like that woman. It must be the competition bringing out this side of my friend. The jealousy was not the best side of her personality, for sure. However, if it got us closer, I could definitely learn to live with it.

CHAPTER FIVE:

Alexa unlocked her elbow from mine before we rounded the privacy fence. That gave me a little concern that perhaps it was just a show of affection to block the other woman's attention, or my interest in Jada. The jealousy was undeniable and was making things a little uncomfortable.

Together we worked silently on removing the scrappy barricade and placed it back immediately after entry. It was certainly good to be back inside. Our new home was shaping up slowly, but we could see the fruits of our efforts already. After coming through the front door of the old Hollywood beer store you now faced a wall of shelving. We placed it there to potentially slow down intruders. To the right was the raised sales counter, behind which we had been sleeping. The path required us to circle around to the left, almost to the back office, to get around our new wall system. Then, we passed through the dining room to reach the kitchen area, which was the old deli section behind the sales counter. Between the dining room and the front door, but still behind the new wall, was our expansive and vacant living room area. The lack of seating there was unmistakable.

"We forgot to get the pews," I muttered quietly to myself.

There were two end tables near the corners of the living area, each with a tall fake potted plant adjacent. A heap of throw pillows and assorted seat cushions sat in the middle of the space. The room was begging for a sofa.

The dining area had a six-foot pine table and six cushioned chairs. There were more mock plants in that room as well, including a plastic flower arrangement as the centerpiece. Alexa immediately headed to the table and sat in one of the ladder-back chairs looking depressed. I pulled out another one across the table from her, turned it around, and sat down with my arms resting on the seat back.

Alexa sat there silently as I watched the blue streaks flash on her forehead and chest. The unusual display was amazing, as it perfectly matched her brilliant blue eyes and never distracted from her natural beauty. Then, I realized, she was reading me. Did she want to know how I felt about her? Or, our new neighbor? I tried to think of something other than the hottie in front of me or the sexy dark-skinned woman in the church.

"We can go back for the pews later, I guess. Hopefully there won't be a bunch of animals in there feasting," I said, trying to make conversation.

"Forget the pews, Mason."

"Okay," I replied. I didn't like her tone so much, but I could understand the temporary seating plan being scrapped, given the circumstances. "So, what would you like to talk about? Is there a question that you would like to ask me? Or, can you already read everything you need to know?"

Alexa's frustration subsided some then, converting over to something more resembling sadness. "Mason, I can't read your mind. I told you that before, it's not like that. However, I can clearly see that you are still very attracted to me and growing fonder of having me around every day." She reached across the table for my hand and I freely gave it to her. It was only the second time that I held her small hand in mine, and I liked it very much. She smiled as she said, "And I like that a lot. However, I could also tell that you found Jada very appealing, too. And, if you don't already know, she likes you at least as much."

I thought back to our brief experience with Jada. I guessed her to be about five foot seven, maybe a hundred and fifty pounds due to her muscle density. She could be in her thirties, but her smooth milk chocolate skin would convince you otherwise. The muscular definition in her chest, arms and legs were captivating, not in the least manly looking. Her breasts, though probably confined significantly by a sports bra, were noticeably larger than Alexa's. I never considered myself to be a breast man, but some things could not go without drawing attention.

"I guess what I'm trying to say is," Alexa confessed. "And this is not easy for me to say, by the way. I'm a little afraid that you might replace me with another woman."

"No," I replied, squeezing her hand. "Alexa, I have no interest in replacing you. I mean, I'm not sure exactly what our relationship is, but I won't let anyone take your place."

"I knew that you would say that. And, I know that you mean it. But I also know that you sometimes can't control how you are feeling, especially about women. Jada would be much more aggressive than me at seeking your affection. I'm not sure that you'd be able to resist her."

"Really?"

"Let me just ask you this," Alexa said, gazing deep into my eyes instead of summoning her gift. "Will you be patient with me? I like you a lot, but I'm slow when it comes to building relationships. Can you promise me that you won't get frustrated and toss me aside? That you won't choose horny over happy?"

"Of course," I answered, reasonably sure that I believed it myself. Though she was right. It was hard to control my emotions around beautiful women. I wanted Alexa to be my girlfriend pretty much more than anything else in this new fucked up world. But how long would I wait if another, just as sexy, woman desired that spot in my life? I wanted to be that man that would fend off other seductive women, but I wasn't sure if I really could be. And should I even? If there was no commitment between us? So far, our situation was kind of one sided.

"Okay," she said slowly, obviously reading my mixed emotions. "Thank you. And thank you for saving my life again in the church. I'm sorry that I didn't mention that earlier. I am truly grateful for how successfully protective that you are."

"What did I do in the church?"

"Mason, you deflected that hatchet that was headed straight for me. How did you not see that? I could sense from you in that exact moment that you would have blocked that blade with your own body to protect me, if necessary, to save my life. I appreciate that so much in you. No, I love that in you. Your power is certainly beyond dodging bullets and blades. You can deflect things that are not even aimed at you."

I had originally thought that the small ax was heading straight for her. I remember that clearly now. Apparently, I had not misjudged its projected course. Alexa was likely correct. Its path had been drastically altered in flight. We had to assume that was my doing. I sat there for a moment coming to terms with it and pondering its possibilities.

"I think we should test it." Alexa said. "I'm serious this time. I mean, the better you understand your skill the more effective job you can do protecting us."

"Agreed."

"Okay, let's get some dinner. I don't know about you, but I'm starving. It will be dark soon, so maybe tomorrow morning we can work on honing your deflection abilities."

It was our first meal sitting at the new dining room table. I was surprised at how much of a difference it made in the atmosphere of the cavernous space. The experience felt so much more civilized with the short dividing walls and sparse decor. We could almost forget about our post-apocalyptic situation for a short time. A light fixture centered above the table would be a huge improvement, though. Perhaps I could rig up a way to hang one of the battery-operated lanterns upside down from the ceiling. Alexa would like that, I think. The more the place resembled a normal home the quicker our relationship would develop. I believed that to be true.

Alexa agreed about the rudimentary chandelier idea and had some other suggestions as well. I still thought the pews would be sufficient for the living room, but she was now dead set against it. I'm sure her reasoning in part was avoiding more contact with the attractive and assertive Jada next door. I believed that it was best that I concede on that one.

We talked extensively about how to improve our bathroom arrangement. Going outside to make a poopy was more dangerous than I liked. Without plumbing, though, indoor options were even less desirable. An outhouse close to the back exit that we could maintain and keep secure would be the best choice. There were a few things we could do in the kitchen to provide better food preparation and cooking possibilities. Now that we had a nice table, I suggested finding a deck of cards and some board games. A little recreation time to reap the rewards of our efforts would be wonderful.

Alexa started yet another shopping list as I settled in, placing my legs across the seat of another ladder-back chair. I was getting much more comfortable with her enchanting presence, rarely gawking at her lithe anatomy lately. When we spoke, I looked into her eyes instead of studying her lovely face. She appeared to be getting more relaxed with me, too. When we settled in for the night, she pulled her bed of blankets right up to next mine. We weren't side by side like lovers, unfortunately, but our heads were close allowing us to talk softly until we fell asleep.

I woke just before Alexa the following day, but she insisted that she be allowed to prepare the coffee and breakfast. Doing her fair share of the work was important to her. For me, her exquisite company was all I needed. Rummaging around the building for items that could be used for future projects, I separated them from the pure junk. In time, I would discard most of that rubbish outside. Maybe stack it close to the doors to discourage anyone from checking this place out more closely.

Alexa alerted me that coffee was ready, so I joined her at the table. We were still waiting on some canned sausage to heat up. Just as my ass hit the brown leather cushion, her face flashed blue causing her to look toward the entrance. Then, there was a rattling knock at some sheet metal in front of the door.

"Hello! Mason? Are you guys in there?"

"Jada?" I said in a low voice, surprised and intrigued at the same time.

"Dammit!" Alexa muttered quietly. Turning to me she said, "Can you get rid if her, Mason?"

"That's not nice, Alexa. Let me see what she wants. Maybe she needs help." I walked around the five-foot tall beer walls we had arranged to reach the front entrance. I didn't want to have to yell any louder than necessary. "Jada? Is that you?"

"Mason! Yes, it's me, Jada, from the church. Can I come in?"

I looked back at Alexa's reaction to the request. She was now standing rigid by the dining table with her arms crossed, shaking her head no. Turning Jada away didn't seem right to me. However, I didn't want to upset my roommate. I had to play this as delicately as I could. It was not my skill set.

"What's wrong?" I asked our unexpected visitor.

"They came back for me," she replied. "I got away from them by going the long way around the fence, through the neighborhood. I didn't lead them to you. I'm sure of it. Can I please come in?" Then, after a long pause with no response from us. "Alexa, can I please come in? I won't cause any trouble, I promise."

Alexa then took a heavy sigh, dropped her arms, then nodded. Jada addressing her directly was a good move. No doubt, she knew much more about how Alexa was thinking than I was.

"Okay," I told Jada. "Start moving the debris from your side, and I'll work on my end." Less than a minute later she was inside the building helping me stack everything back securely. It was obvious that her strength in lifting the barricade objects was near my own. I was impressed. I couldn't help but check out her muscular form as we worked together. Then, I remembered that Alexa would know much of what I was thinking based on the emotions she sensed. I shifted my thoughts to how I could improve our entrance set up.

"Thank you," Jada said to me, once our task was complete and I began guiding her around the short walls. Then she addressed my companion. "Thank you, Alexa. I appreciate your hospitality."

Alexa gave our guest a blank stare with her arms crossed again. This time, even her hips had an attitude. Jada would not know about Alexa's gift. I almost felt it would only be fair to warn her, but that certainly wouldn't go over well with my roommate. I'm sure Alexa wanted to keep her special talent a secret. I couldn't blame her. It was assuredly a strong defensive asset.

Jada was wearing the same workout clothes as I vividly remembered the day before, and still smoking hot in them. Additionally, she carried a large backpack behind her and a long weapons bag from one arm. It looked like she had enough time to grab all her stuff before she scooted out of the church where she'd been hiding. Maybe it was her intention to try to move in with us ever since we left her yesterday. There was no sure way to confirm her story, unless the skunk horde shows up at our door soon to support it.

At this point, Jada and Alexa were still separated by the shelving obstructions, and I was on Jada's side. I figured that was a bad idea. Best to get closer to my partner soon. I looked Jada over for recent wounds, but didn't see any?

"Are you okay?" I asked. "Did you get injured?"

"No, thanks for asking. I actually got out of there before they could get to me."

"Well," I said. "Why don't you set your gear down here for now. You can join us at the table. Do you like coffee?"

"Oh my God!" Jada exclaimed. "You guys have coffee?"

"Yes. Alexa just made a fresh pot. We should have plenty to share."

"I'll fix you a cup," Alexa said flatly. "Here, have a seat."

The darker skinned woman sat down elegantly and crossed her legs. I had the impression that she would be comfortable at an expensive restaurant. To avoid gawking at her remarkable physical attributes I took a seat across the table from her and returned intently to my cup of Joe. It was still hot. Alexa returned with a full green cup for our guest. I knew we had four of the white mugs that we were using. She must have decided Jada's shouldn't match us.

"Thank you, dear," Jada said with what appeared to me to be genuine appreciation. I was glad to see that she was working to soften up Alexa's attitude toward her. I believed it was going to be harder than she could ever imagine, given Alexa's secret ability.

My blond friend then surprised me a little by standing beside me. She leaned her slim frame up against me while placing her arm casually around my shoulders. I took the liberty of reciprocating by looping my left arm around her sexy thin thighs. I tried to act natural sipping my coffee while gently stroking the smooth skin of her bare her leg. She did not flinch, so I continued. The scene appeared to have the desired effect on our guest as she glanced between us.

"Thank you both for letting me in," Jada said. "I know it's hard these days to trust anyone. The two of you have a nice thing going on here. A nice place for a nice couple. Have you been together since before the plague?"

Alexa squeezed my shoulder. I knew that she wanted to put on a show of an unbreakable bond in front of our provocative new friend. I was all for it, especially if it rapidly advanced our relationship. I could get used to holding her in my arms.

"No," I answered. I didn't believe in outright lying if it wasn't totally necessary. Lies seemed to have a way of coming back to bite you in the ass later. However, I was a big fan of stretching the truth when it was appropriate. Make a relationship that's only days old seem like it has been months. "We found each other since then and hit it off. We've been inseparable since. Why don't you tell us more about yourself?"

"Ok, that's fair," she responded, nodding. "Well, I was married with two children, Tyler and Kasey. I lost them all to the plague."

"Why do you call it a plague? Wasn't it a bunch of different diseases?" Alexa asked.

"I don't know the right term, I guess. But you are right. There were dozens of diseases released when the earth heated up after the comet struck in Asia. The ice melted everywhere and dead animals that were centuries old thawed out, still harboring viruses from their time. Our bodies never had a chance against them. The governments struggled to make headway on a virus just to have two or three more start killing people. So very few were immune. No doubt you both are like me. We had to watch helplessly as our friends and family died."

A tear formed in Jada's eye as she spoke. For a few moments we sat there in silence, as if showing respect for our lost loved ones. I felt Alexa's body slump against me. She was softening up toward Jada. The genuine grief that she sensed from the woman must have helped.

"So, how old are you?" Alexa eventually asked. I thought it was rude for women to ask each other their age, but in this new society those niceties seemed to have faded away.

"I'm thirty-three, dear," Jada replied without hesitation. "My children were just four and two. My husband, Jeff was my age. We owned a couple gyms together. They were doing okay. I also had a fitness training video business, called Jada Fitness. I was just getting that started when all this happened. These workout clothes were practically all that I took with me when I left. Fortunately, I have four identical sets to change between. My house was being looted when I got home from the hospital after my baby passed away. I wasn't able to grab anything else without taking a serious risk. With the extreme heat we've been having, I figured it would be enough."

"It's a nice outfit," Alexa said. "You look very attractive in it."

"Thank you, sweetheart. That's very sweet of you to say. I know I am intruding here, but I thought I'd give it a chance before I wander away from the area. I'm good with weapons. I can help provide protection and do some hunting. I don't snore in my sleep. I'm happy to help with any odd jobs that need doing. Do you think you two have room for a third?"

CHAPTER SIX:

"What do you think?" I asked Alexa. I had pulled her to the back office of the store so we could speak privately. I assumed that she would be fiercely opposed to the new roommate request of Jada. And she probably knew that I would be in favor of it. Not just because I would be living with two gorgeous women. The addition of the dark warrior could strengthen our defenses. And contribute significantly to our overall work production. However, I was also stoked about my romantic progress with Alexa and didn't want to mess that up. Honestly, though, Alexa had become closer to me because of Jada. So, it could truly be a win-win for me.

"I don't know what to think," she whispered. "On one hand, we'd be much stronger with her. That is, of course, if we can trust her. On the other hand, I don't know if I will be able to tolerate her presence very well. We have a good thing going already, don't we? I'm afraid that adding her might ruin our situation."

I was delighted that she was thinking logically. Her thoughts were not fully clouded by her emotions. I believed that would work in Jada's favor.

"Well, what do you sense from her? Is she trustworthy?"

"Oh, I sense plenty from her alright," Alexa smirked. "I don't think she will try to kill us in our sleep or steal our stuff. But she's got the hots for you, Mason. Big time! I don't know if I can compete with her."

"It's not a competition, Alexa. You and I are sort of in a relationship. It's very early for us, true, but still. I'm not going to let another woman break us up. Don't worry about that."

"Mason," she said, looking me straight in the eye. "There are a lot more women left alive then men. She won't be only attractive survivor that will take an interest in you. Believe me."

"So, what do we do?"

"I don't know. If I decide, it might be based solely on how I feel about you. What is the logical decision?" Alexa asked. I still couldn't believe she was interested in logic in this situation. That showed a maturity beyond her years in my opinion. I respected that. It was a quality that I found very appealing in a mate as well.

"Without a doubt, the logical decision would be to take her in," I replied confidently. "The only issue would be trust, but I'll rely on your intuition for that. Are you clearing her as a threat?"

Alexa peeked back into the room at Jada, but she could only see the top of her head over the beer shelving. The mixed braids with red coloring and string remained motionless. I didn't know if visibility improved Alexa's readings or not, but I waited patiently for her response.

Finally, she nodded and said. "Yes. I just don't trust her with my man."

"Your man, huh?"

She placed her hand on my chest as she smiled up at me with pouting lips. Her head then rest against my shoulder as she whispered, "I don't want you alone with her."

"Works for me." When she pulled her head back, I gently tilted up her dainty chin with my hand. I glanced quickly between her eyes and her lips, hoping that I was clearly communicating what I wanted to do. Then, very softly, I placed my lips against hers for a moment. My eyes instinctively closed when I kissed her. I was happy to see that her eyes were still closed when I reopened mine. The show of affection was unquestionably accepted and appreciated.

I kept my arm around the tapered small section of her back as we casually returned to the dining area. Jada didn't look like she had moved an inch while she was waiting for our response. I knew from her manner that when she asked to join us, she was not incredibly optimistic that we would agree. I believe that she doubted that my jealous girlfriend would accept her. She certainly had good reason to feel that way.

"Oh, my," Jada said as we approached the table smiling. Our joyful expression was mostly afterglow from our kiss, but she didn't know that. She stood up hastily in her excitement, nearly knocking the chair backwards to the floor. "It looks like you are going to say yes."

"Yes," I replied. "We have agreed that you would be a great addition to our team. Welcome to your new home."

"Yay," Jada said enthusiastically. It looked like she was itching to give me a hug. Though I would welcome it, my partner would no doubt take offense. Fortunately, she turned to Alexa first and wrapped her arms firmly around thinner woman. It took Alexa by surprise, but she quickly joined in the celebratory embrace. I was delighted to see a wide grin on her face as she turned to me. When Jada pulled away, she asked Alexa, "Is it okay if I give Mason a quick thank you hug?"

Blue flashed across Alexa's forehead and chest briefly before she nodded her approval. I was careful to keep my hands in the safe zone as I hugged our new roommate. Her grip was firm, but quick. When she released, her hands remained on my biceps for another moment.

"You are a strong man in your own right, Mason," Jada said with a sparkle in her eye. "I have weapons to share, and I can train you if you want. You, too, Alexa."

"Oh, that's okay," Alexa said. "I'll let you two do most of the fighting, if you don't mind. I would be worthless in battle beside both of you."

"Don't sell yourself short, girl," Jada said warmly. I was glad to see her working to befriend Alexa quickly. "I'm sure that you have talents in areas well beyond mine. We'll make a good team, I think."

Alexa spent the next few minutes showing our new friend around the place and explaining our current routine. When we finally sat back down at the table to finish our coffee we talked some more. Sadly, we forgot about the sausage cooking. It was more like burnt jerky by the time we remembered. Alexa grabbed a box of sweet pastries that we had been saving for a special occasion. The things must have been pumped full of preservatives to still be edible after all that time. We shared with Jada our plans to improve our dwelling. She had some good ideas as well but was carefully wording everything she said to show the respect that she had as the newcomer. I was gaining even more confidence in our decision to accept her.

"Do you guys mind if I clear a space in the back corner for exercise and weapons training?" Jada asked.

"Not at all," I replied, visualizing our new friend working out. Her firm round butt filled out the tight spandex shorts wonderfully. "I can help move things around."

"Maybe put some walls around it for her privacy," Alexa interjected. Again, I wondered if she had read my very specific thoughts. She had been vague all along about her gift's capacity. If it was possible that she could literally read my thoughts, did she see what I was imagining? Did my visual of Jada's high-quality ass appear in her mind?

"Thank you, dear," Jada nodded to Alexa. "I also like to wash up every day, but I can fetch the extra water for that myself."

"I think a daily sponge bath would be good for all of us," Alexa replied, elbowing me gently. I wasn't quite diligent with my personal care before the girls came along. I did need to change that, especially if I would be getting some cuddle time with Alexa soon. Water was so precious that we needed to find a way to maximize its effectiveness when bathing so we don't waste any. My mind wandered once again to the two beautiful women soaping up their bodies. I glanced at Alexa to see if she was reacting to my thoughts. I didn't see the telltale blue flashes or any expected reaction, though.

"I've started on a neighborhood map," I changed the subject, just in case. "I'll mark what houses that we've already raided for supplies, and any hazards I've encountered so far. You can mark the places that you've been as well, Jada. We have a little wagon, but I wouldn't mind finding something that could hold more."

We continued to discuss our plans for more supply runs, and Alexa's growing shopping list. I helped Jada with moving the beer shelving around in the back corner to make a suitable exercise room. There was a lot of product on the floor, and broken glass too, so it took a while to completely clean it up. Alexa started on an early lunch so we could head out for supplies around noon. As I was scooping up debris to place in a trash can, I heard Jada call my name. When I turned to face her, I was alarmed to find a small blue ball heading straight for me. It struck me in the chest before I could respond. The dense racquetball kind of hurt a little when it hit.

"Hey!" I yelled out, catching the ball in my hand as it dropped. I wasn't angry enough to whip it back at her, but it was annoying. "What the hell, Jada?"

"Sorry," she apologized. "I was just testing your reflexes. You moved really well during the battle in the church. I thought maybe it was a reflex thing."

I looked over to Alexa as she was working in the dining area. She was placing food on the table and overheard us. She shook her head no ever so slightly, indicating that she didn't want me to reveal my special deflection ability just yet. I could appreciate her reasoning. However, Jada could be instrumental in assisting me understand and hone my skills. Additionally, revealing my gift could encourage her to tell us about any special talents that she might have. I decided to wait until a better moment to have that discussion. I tossed the dense ball back to her without a word. I could tell that she was expecting there to be more to the conversation.

After our energizing meal we gathered up our bags, wagon, and some weapons before heading out. Alexa reluctantly took my baseball bat. She was still too scared to handle anything with a blade. Jada carried her trusty spear and handed me the hatchet with which I was already familiar. I slid the handle through a belt loop of my cargo shorts to keep my hand free as I pulled the small wagon. Our plan was to scavenge methodically from house to house this time, crossing them off the map. There was a slew of homes on the next couple streets to the south that I had not checked out yet. We decided to make our way in that direction.

Jada announced that she would scout ahead for any possible issues. I almost told her that Alexa's ability was a better method, then remembered we didn't want to reveal that just yet. Also, it didn't work on animals, apparently.

"How far away can you sense people?" I asked Alexa as Jada started pulling ahead.

"I don't know, maybe a couple hundred feet?"

"Jada," I raised my voice hoping not to be overheard by possible enemies. "Try to stay within a hundred feet of us, for communication."

She nodded then ducked around the back of a house facing our street. We would have to cut through some backyards to make if over to the next street. If not for the wagon it would be best to stay behind the buildings. However, fences and uneven ground made that nearly impossible if we wanted to cart supplies back. Before we reached that same corner, Jada reappeared and said the area was clear. We made it to the first house on our list successfully without incident.

The home was a small one-story rancher with a basement. The yellow vinyl siding was turning brown, making it almost the same color as the faded shutters. Both the front and back doors seemed secure. Basement door in the back did, too. Jada circled the house looking for broken windows as I began working on prying open the rear door. As instructed, Alexa stayed with the wagon at the bottom of the five concrete steps, one hand resting on the wrought iron handrail. Her face flashed blue periodically as she tried to determine if there was anyone inside or around the building. Jada returned just as I got the door jimmied open. The confident dark workout queen entered first, then Alexa as I looked around for anyone possibly watching us enter. Everything was smooth so far.

The modest home was a bit of a mess, but I believed that was how the residents had kept it. There were tons of dirty dishes, newspapers, and clothes lying everywhere. No rodents visible yet, but there were plenty of insects. We found almost a full case of bottled water, some crackers and canned food, as well as a bit of medical supplies. We returned to the back door quickly, not wanting to stay in there any longer than necessary.

Alexa approached the exit first and paused briefly to perform her sweep of the area. A minute later all the items were in the cart as we headed for the next house over. This one had a three-foot high chain link fence around the back yard with two decaying animal carcasses, probably dogs. More insects, too. We decided to try the front door instead. Both girls cleared us for entry into the white two-story brick home. The front door was closed but unlocked. We treaded carefully just in case, but there was no one in there. More water and bag snacks. Not much of anything else of value.

Jada reached the front door first, then turned to Alexa and asked, "Did you want to do your thing before we go out?" The two girls stared at each other for a moment, Alexa registering that our new friend already knew she had a special ability. Alexa nodded as the beautiful blue streaks flashed on her temples and chest, then she pointed at the door.

"Okay, I guess that's out of the way," I whispered as we loaded up the wagon.

"We can talk more about it when we get back," Jada said. "And your kinetic battle ability, too. "

"My what?"

"That thing you do when the veins in your arms turn colors as you redirect objects like my ax. Did you think I didn't notice that?"

"Alright," I conceded. "You can then share with us any special abilities that you have."

"To my knowledge," she replied. "I don't have any. Unless you count my awesome fighting skills and sexual prowess." The temptress then gave me a seductive smile. I turned to Alexa to see her response, both from Jada's denial of extra talent and her flirting.

Alexa just shrugged, then said calmly, "I think she's telling the truth. Unless she's acquired an edge in combat, any special ability she might have gained has not manifested itself yet."

We decided to return our focus to the task at hand and table this discussion for later. The third house in the row had been consumed by fire, and the fourth one too damaged by it to make entry safe. We then crossed the narrowly paved street with caution to try the houses on the other side before calling it quits for the day. A neat cape cod with blue siding looked to be relatively untouched. There was a glass enclosed porch on the front with the door unlocked. The small space was vacant except for a pair of women's boots and two packages that had been delivered long ago but never opened. Without hesitation I ripped the tape off to find some men's crew socks, a USB memory stick, and some white chocolate nut energy bars. The latter went straight to the cart.

Jada threw her sturdy shoulder into the painted metal front door while I was busy opening my presents. Her third try busted the frame and sent the door swinging into the wall. If anyone was home, they would certainly know that we're there. I lifted the wagon into the enclosed porch to make it less noticeable to anyone passing by. The three of us then began our search. Again, more water and snacks. A stock pile of energy and nutrition bars was a huge find. We decided to grab more cutlery and dishes, too. There was also a clean blue tarp folded up in the corner of the laundry room. I decided to drape it over our wagon full of goods. Before we leave, I could tuck it in on all sides to keep the load secure as I pulled the small wheels across uneven terrain.

The home wasn't huge, but it was nice inside with plank style flooring throughout. The furniture and wall decor were tasteful, and it was very clean. One of the bedrooms had been converted into an exercise room with a treadmill, rowing machine, and some free weights. Jada grabbed some of the lighter barbells and a couple foam mats. Then, we decided to check the closets for clothes that might fit us, since these people must have been in good shape. Before we could get far into our wardrobe shopping there was a pounding on the glass out front. We all froze simultaneously.

The thumping continued, though it was not loud. I peeked out the second story bedroom window to see maybe twenty stinkies in the front yard. They appeared to be passing through when one of the skanks noticed the wagon on the porch. She was drawing the attention of the others as well. Shit! We didn't want to have to fight them, but we also didn't want to lose all the good supplies we stacked up in the cart. The three of us watched through the thin green bedroom curtains as the scene unfolded below.

Grunted communication took place among several of them until the lone skunk left his lead position. He decided to check out what the fuss was about at the glass enclosure. Three skanks were then pointing at the wagon or tapping on the glass like children picking out what they wanted at an old-time candy store. One of the other skanks, a huge one, maybe the biggest I have seen so far, searched the ground until she found a large rock about the size of her head. She could barely lift it. Apparently, she planned to smash through the glass barrier, even though I was pretty sure we left the porch door unlocked.

The skunk was a middle eastern man wearing ragged tight blue three-quarter pants with his rashy ankles exposed. He had on a Washington Capitals red t-shirt while sporting a purple Baltimore Ravens ball cap. These sick people maintained some of their humanity, but obviously none of their fashion sense. As I almost chuckled from the thought, he looked right up at us. My two female companions closed the curtains quickly, but it was too late. He had seen us already. I continued watching to see what he would do.

Just then there was a collective growl from the street below and responsive shrieking from half of the skanks. A small pack of wild dogs was headed their way. The focus of the decadent horde quickly shifted from us and our wagon to the approaching predators. The group of five scraggly beasts looked like wolves in their formation as they pressed the stinkies back slowly toward the house. Oversized claws and fangs were obvious on the canines, even from our viewpoint. The alpha male may have literally been a black wolf from its appearance. His green eyes glowed eerily on the cloudy day. I urged the girls to return to the windows to watch with me how this played out.

The skunk grabbed a wooden walking cane off the front lawn. I hadn't seen it there before. Perhaps one of the skanks had dropped it. He raised it above his head in a threatening pose as he slowly worked his way through his female followers toward the dogs. The skank in the very front stood motionless, as if entranced by the lead wolf's emerald stare.

When one of the rabid-like dogs from the side dove for the still woman, the hefty skank stepped forward. She crushed its head with the rock she had been holding. Wow! I had never seen one of the decaying humans move so fast or fight so strong. The pack was shaken by the quick loss of one of their own, but they did not retreat. When the big skank reached for the rock again two more dogs attacked her before she could lift it. She didn't go down right away despite large chunks of flesh being torn from her pale gray body. A couple other rotten women tried to come to her rescue only to be taken down speedily by the other dogs. Mister skunk then rallied his survivors and made for an escape. Their crippled forms scurried off, disjointed in their hurry like a geriatric race to the bathroom. The slowest of them was then snagged from behind by the green-eyed alpha male.

The sound of ripping flesh and bone crunching reached us through the upstairs windows. It was a sickening sound threatening to bring up my lunch. With the horde of stinkies gone our wagon should be safe. It was unlikely the wolf pack would try to enter the house. Besides, they were too busy feasting on the rotting flesh of their kills. We decided to sit in the bedroom patiently and wait out the disgusting meal, avoiding drawing any attention to ourselves. Unless one of the dogs had super hearing, we should be okay to talk quietly amongst ourselves.

"Well, that was disturbing," I said as I lowered my ass to the floor. My two sexy female cohorts sat down as well, forming a triangle close enough to hold hands. Alexa grabbed mine, fear and tears apparent in her eyes. No doubt, she sensed the fear from the sub human people as they tried to fight off the dogs. Surprisingly, she then reached for Jada's hand. The dark beauty gladly gave it to her, then reached for mine to complete the circle.

"I feel so bad for those people," Alexa said.

"The zombies?" Jada asked in surprise.

"They're not zombies," Alexa replied before I could. "They are alive. They are just very sick and cannot heal. I can feel their emotions. They are not near as complicated as our feelings, though. That many of them scared for their lives all at once was overwhelming."

"So, that's what you do?" Jada asked. "You sense emotions?"

Alexa nodded, her eyes watery from the experience. I saw Jada give the smaller girl's hand a gentle sympathetic squeeze.

"Well, in that case, I feel like shit," Jada confessed. "I've killed more than a few of them. It was in self-defense, but I didn't think twice about it. Maybe we can avoid them more in the future, or hope they'll be hesitant to attack a group of three people with weapons. If they are still real people, I don't want to hurt them unless it is necessary."

"I agree," I said, giving both hands a gentle squeeze.

"The beasts, though," Jada continued. "I won't hesitate to kill them still. They are wild and dangerous. It won't be liking taking the life of someone's pet. Please tell me that you can't feel their pain, Alexa."

"No, thank goodness."

We chatted a little more about the skunks, skanks, and animals. Though the diseases that plagued the humans causing them to decay but not die appeared to all be similar. The animals, though, showed a variety of sicknesses as well as mutations. Jada described some animals that were crazy fast. Others seemed to be able to put people in a deadly trance, like the green-eyed dog. We figured there might even be more types of deviations that we haven't seen yet.

"I once joined a gang," Jada said quietly.

"A gang?" we both asked.

"Yeah, after society broke down, of course. In fact, it was just a couple weeks ago. I was only with them for a few days. These gangs always have one guy in charge, and he tends to have a special ability, just like you Mason. The gang members were mostly females, and a few of them had gifts as well. The man I followed called himself Spark. He was able to produce an electrical charge with his hands. It wasn't like lightning bolts shot out. He could effectively electrify the golf club that he used as a weapon to increase damage. I once saw him shock people that were standing in water. Another time he turned on appliances briefly just to show off."

"Why did you leave?" I asked.

"He was killed by a much larger gang. Their leader was super quick, but only in short spurts. It was a huge advantage in one on one combat, though. But he was a real asshole. The way he acted during and after the battle was absolutely ridiculous. Some of the women from our gang joined him when Spark died. Apparently, that is the new custom. The winner gets the bitches. Some of us just ran. I was with one of the other girls for a few hours. Her name was Riley. She seemed kind of nice, just real quiet. Then we were split up when a deranged flock of geese attacked us. That there was some crazy shit to see, let me tell you. We ran separate ways seeking shelter. I couldn't find her after that. I'm assuming she is still alive. I sincerely hope that she is."

"Do you want to search for her?" Alexa asked.

"Kind of," Jada replied. "But I doubt that I'll find her. It's best to stay with you two and focus on our own survival, I think. She might have joined another one of those gangs by now."

As we waited for an opportunity to exit safely, I gathered some games for us to play in our down time back at our place. The family that owned this house must have been game night people, because they had a wide variety of card and board games. I found two poker size decks of cards, but no chips for betting. I always wanted to have a poker night with my friends, back when they were still alive. I didn't know if Alexa and Jada would like to play or not.

A little while later we headed back to the old store. The dogs had eaten their fill of the dead skanks in the front yard and wandered off. The odor left behind was beyond nauseating and required that we make a wide berth. It was twilight by that time, but the journey was thankfully uneventful. Jada and I sorted our newly acquired supplies while Alexa started on dinner. She opened three cans of chunky soup and a new box of crackers. We had some leftover cheese from the deli to compliment the meal. Despite the heat, the taste of the soup was wonderful compared to many of the rations.

After cleaning ourselves up we decided to play some of the newly acquired games. A unique card game named Castles & Catapults was very entertaining. We played four games before deciding to move onto something else. A little playful feud had developed between the two women because they kept stealing each other's gold in the game. That's when I told them about my desire to play poker.

"Unfortunately, we don't have anything to use for poker chips," I said.

"Who needs chips," Jada replied enthusiastically. "Strip poker is more fun anyway."

"You must be in a hurry to get naked," I laughed. "I'm a decent poker player."

"No, but I'm the only one here that hasn't seen you naked, I assume." Jada glanced at Alexa for a reaction. The blue flashed across her skin ever so briefly as she stiffened up. She gave no verbal response.

"Okay, okay," I said. "Maybe we should play something else. How about gin rummy?"

I explained the rules and the girls agreed to play. Before we started, Alexa grabbed two bottles of wine that she had set aside for a special occasion. I poured a generous dose in three newly acquired coffee mugs, each representing a different beach town. I had Ocean City. I handed Myrtle Beach to Jada and Atlantic City to Alexa. By the time we finished the first bottle I was feeling quite mellow, but Alexa was nearly drunk. Her slight form couldn't handle the alcohol as well as our more muscular friend.

It wasn't long before we gave up on the card game and started talking about what we missed most from the old world. It was surprising the things that really mattered. Your own bed. A meaningful routine. Working toilets. A job to keep you focused and productive. Fresh fruit & vegetables, of course. And meat. We all missed that protein source that was so taken for granted before. Jada talked about hunting and how much work it would be to clean the kill properly before cooking. I had never hunted before but was willing to learn. I imagined it would be an important survival skill from now on. Alexa wasn't near as enthusiastic about cleaning and cooking the dead animals, though.

I pushed back from the table to stretch my legs as we continued our relaxed conversation. Alexa poured herself another cup of wine despite my warning, then sat across my lap with her arm around my shoulders. I didn't hesitate to place my arms around her sexy slender body, though in part it was to keep her from falling off. It was not my style to take advantage of drunk women, but Alexa claimed to be my girlfriend. Caressing her long smooth legs and the bare skin of her lower back seemed acceptable to me. When she turned the other way, I often glanced at her small but firm breasts trapped under her tight t-shirt and thin bra. As I wondered how far I should take things tonight I couldn't help but get aroused. Alexa responded playfully by shifting on my lap and kissing my cheek.

Finally, Jada declared it was time for bed. Her flirtatious nature had faded with Alexa's display of affection. She had arranged some foam pads and a thick blanket in the exercise area for her bedding. After guiding Alexa around the sales counter to our sleeping area I was pleased to see her pull her bed beside mine to form one large bed for the two of us. I kissed her softly on her forehead as she snuggled in on my chest. A few seconds later she was asleep, looking angelic and peaceful. I had hoped for more touching and smooching but considering her inebriated condition I figured this was probably for the best. With the girl of my dreams in my arms I eventually drifted off as well, to have the most restful night of sleep that I'd had in many months.

CHAPTER SEVEN:

The heavy thunderstorm rolled in just before the sun came up. The sound of lightning and pelting rain against the windows woke me early. Alexa remained groggy from the night of drinking and snuggled into my body under a thin blanket. Her beautiful face rested peacefully on my chest as her left thigh stretched across my waist. My left arm that was pinned under her light frame wrapped around her shoulders, holding her close to me. I slid my right hand under the blanket to softly caress the smooth skin of her leg as she slept. I had never held such a desirable girl before. Truth was my romantic encounters had been quite limited before the big catastrophe. It took the world ending for me to gain such a prize as Alexa. Not only was she gorgeous, I had become endeared to her layered personality as well. I couldn't remember another girl as lovable as the one I held to me in my bed at that moment.

Another crash of thunder jarred Alexa awake, sounding shortly after the flash of light through the cracks in the boarded windows. That one was close. I hoped that the lightning would not spark any fires that couldn't be immediately doused out by the pouring rain. My girl opened her eyes to look up at me as I kissed her gently on the forehead. I could see that she was disoriented for a couple seconds, like shaking the fog from the dream that she was just having. I pulled back my hands to give her some space as she woke up.

"Is it storming?" she asked as she laid her head back down on my chest and welcomed my embrace.

"Yeah, the rain is coming down pretty hard out there." It had been several weeks since any significant rainfall. I wasn't sure if this downpour was progress on mother nature's part, or a sign of bad things to come.

"Is Jada okay?"

"I don't know, I just woke up a couple minutes ago."

"You should go check on her," Alexa said, sliding off me to free up my arm.

I slept in my shorts but no t-shirt. I figured there was a good chance that Jada was still asleep, so I didn't bother to cover my bare chest. The only working clock we had sat on the sales counter. In the dim light of the small lantern we left on overnight it looked like it read about five thirty in the morning. It was still very early. If it wasn't for the storm, I would have slept for at least another two hours.

I tip-toed my way through the store toward the section where Jada had claimed for her exercise area and bedroom. She had a small lantern on there as well. I don't remember if it was on when I went to bed. As I approached her section, I saw a shadow move on the wall. Apparently, she was awake. It wasn't until I got closer that I realized what she was doing. She had just pulled on a pair of her tight shorts, but there was nothing covering her upper body. I couldn't make out the details of her breasts, except that they were round and large. I stopped in my tracks and held my breath, not wanting to be caught peeping on her, even if it was accidental. I ought to turn around and go back to Alexa, but I couldn't quite pull my eyes away.

Jada then slid a sports bra over her head and pulled it down into place, pressing those impressive chocolate melons in tight. When she reached for her shirt, that's when I noticed that she saw me.

"Mason?" She didn't seem shocked, or embarrassed. Modesty was probably not a personality trait of hers. It was understandable. Most men would find this woman smoking hot, especially if they were into the athletic type.

"Sorry, I was just coming to check on you because of the storm. You okay?"

"Sure, I'm fine," she replied as she pulled on her tight red shirt with the Jada Fitness logo in the center. "The storm woke me up. I figured I'd go ahead and get cleaned up and changed. I like the shirtless look on you. You have a nice chest."

"Oh, thanks," I replied, tempted to cover myself. Instead, I just stood there motionless as she walked right up to me. We locked eyes in the dim light as she placed her small hands on my chest, then slid them up to my shoulders then down my arms. Jada then licked her lips as she stared at my mouth. That's when I snapped out of it. I was almost entranced enough to kiss her, if she were so inclined. It certainly looked like she was. Her touch was magic on my body, like a sexy masseuse.

"O-okay," I stuttered, pulling back and turning to see of Alexa was watching.

"It's not fair, Mason."

"What's not fair?"

"That Alexa gets to keep you for herself. There are so few men left in this world. And most of them are not good men like you. She needs to share." She stepped forward and reached like she was going to touch the front of my shorts. I jumped back, but part of me undeniably desired the contact. I believed that she knew that to be the case. She flashed me an evil smile before she turned back around and bent over to grab her socks and shoes. The sight of her round ass and strong legs got me breathing a little heavier. I practically ran back to Alexa.

"Is she okay?" Alexa asked. Thank goodness that she had not seen what happened. I did my best not to respond to Jada's advance, but it might not have looked that way from Alexa's viewpoint.

"Yeah, she's fine. She's already awake." I avoided thinking about Jada or feeling guilty in case Alexa would pick up on it. If she did sense anything in me, I wanted it to be my attraction to my girlfriend. I slid back under the thin blanket and put my arm around her.

"Do you want me to make coffee?" Alexa asked.

"No, I think I prefer to lay here with you."

Alexa smiled and placed her chin on my chest. I pulled her close and gave her a firm kiss. She seemed to melt in my arms, so I continued. I never studied how to be a good kisser, so I just let my passion for this young woman guide me. She responded well as I varied my position and pressure, using my tongue on occasion. Alexa's tongue was small but active. Before long she had me moaning softly into her mouth. When she adjusted her position to lie directly on top of me there was no confusion about my arousal. It seemed to turn her on even more, so I took a chance and slid my hands down her back to gently grip her tight little ass. If felt so good, but I could tell I was getting too carried away. Soon after that we broke the lip lock with a mutual gasp.

"Okay," Alexa whispered as she sat up and removed my hands from her butt. "Slow down cowboy. That was fun, but I think I need to pace myself. I hope you understand."

"No!" That's what I thought anyway. I wanted more, of course. Who wouldn't? She no doubt sensed that I felt that way. There was no hiding it from her. However, it wasn't like she led me on and needed to follow through. She was just taking the next step in showing her affection. I should be glad that my advance was received as well as it was.

"Sure," is all I said.

Alexa sat beside me and looked at my shorts. "Are you going to be okay?"

"Yes, I'll be fine. Let's just lay here together for a few more minutes." It wasn't long before we were talking about what to do if it was going to be raining all day. We had some projects for inside the store. More cleaning and rearranging. I also wanted to do some exercise. I had gotten away from any sort of athletic routine since the world went to shit. Alexa also reminded me that we should be testing my special deflection ability to understand it better. Knowledge in that area could one day make the difference between life and death.

After breakfast I recruited Jada to help me with some manual work. She didn't struggle with lifting and pushing heavy objects like Alexa. From what I could tell, she appreciated the opportunity to work her already impressive muscles.

The rain continued to come down hard, but the lightning had stopped. I checked the perimeter to make sure we wouldn't get flooded out of our home. So far, the elevation of the concrete floor was high enough to keep out the river of rain water that was starting to form in the parking lot. I couldn't see all the way over to the main road. The slope was slight in this area, so I figured that we shouldn't have any raging rapids.

All three of us did some workouts and stretching after breakfast. Jada guided us through a cardio program that felt taxing on my body. Alexa tried her best to keep up, but she had to take more breaks to avoid exhaustion.

"Sorry, I can't exercise as hard as you two," Alexa said to me as we paused for a drink of water. "Jada's body is much better than mine."

"No," I replied. "You are just made differently. Believe me, there is nothing about your body to be ashamed of. You know that I love you just the way you are."

"Thanks," she replied timidly. Then a few seconds later, "so you love me, do you?"

"Well, it was meant as a figure of speech, but yes. Alexa, I am growing very fond of you." I was hesitant to repeat the L word.

"I'm growing very fond of you, too," she replied smiling as she leaned in for a kiss. One day soon we'll have to confess that we are falling in love. When we released the embrace, I saw Jada looking longingly at us out of the corner of her eye.

I was about to apologize to the dark beauty but decided against it. She decided to join us. She would have to deal responsibly with our relationship. Though I could clearly understand the struggle with sexual urges. I ought to be more understanding when she flirted with me, but I absolutely didn't want to send the wrong signal. That would only make matters worse.

During lunch we talked about what we knew of my ability so far. I had dodged a sword and a bullet when fighting Earl. Alexa had witnessed that, so we believed it to be true. Then, I deflected the hatchet that Jada threw at Alexa. According to both women there was no denying that was me. The ball that Jada tossed at me, though, I had no effect on it. Was it because there was no real danger? Or, was it due to the composition of the object? Perhaps, I could only deflect metal. We made a list of tests that would not be too dangerous. I told Alexa I wanted her to stay out of the exercise area when we did them, but she insisted on being nearby.

"Okay," Jada said. "Let's try the ball again." She threw it hard at my chest, but I was expecting it this time. Instead of defecting or dodging it, I instinctively caught it with one hand. "Nice catch," she said. "But that's not what we are trying to do here. Let me throw it at Alexa instead."

"What?" my girlfriend said.

"No," I snapped. "I don't want to take a chance on her getting hurt."

"From a rubber ball?" Jada asked annoyingly.

"Let her hold a piece of cardboard to protect herself."

When Alexa reached for the broken-down beer box that I handed her, Jada threw the ball at her before she was ready. I quickly tried to stick my hand in the way of the projectile to protect Alexa. She didn't have time to bring the cardboard up to protect herself yet. Instead, she cowered away naturally, preparing to take the hit in her shoulder or back. I wasn't quite able to place my hand in the way fast enough. Fortunately, the ball missed her by maybe one inch.

"What the fuck, Jada!" I yelled, as I comforted Alexa. She was still a little cringed up, but not hurt or terribly offended. I saw the blue flashes on her face and knew she was reading Jada's intentions.

"Well, it worked," Jada responded, like it was a simple matter of fact.

"You are lucky that you missed," I snapped.

"No dear, I didn't miss. I never miss. Mason, you deflected the ball. It doesn't have to be metal, then. Let's try more stuff."

I calmed down and Alexa agreed that we should try more tests to best understand my ability. For the first few attempts I was unable to dodge anything not dangerous thrown at me, but I protected Alexa every time. Jada then taught me some focus exercises to try to harness my ability so I could use it at will. I struggled, but eventually it worked. After an hour or so of practice I was able to dodge or deflect everything directed at me.

"My next question," Jada said, "would be if you could move a stationary object with your ability." We worked at that idea for a while, but nothing panned out. I couldn't make anything move no matter how hard I focused.

"Let me try this," I said as I tossed the ball into the air in front of me. I swung my hand at it like I was going to smack it, handball style. Before I made impact with the object, though, it propelled itself at Jada. It didn't come at her at great speed, so she was easily able to catch it.

She appeared delightfully surprised, though. Finally, some success after all the failed attempts to move something sitting still.

"Okay," she said. "So, it needs to be an object already in motion. What if I toss the ball in front of you from the side?" We tried several angles and had a measure of success each time. Unfortunately, I had very little control. The ball would get projected off at all angles, occasionally knocking beer and wine bottles to the floor. Alexa cleaned them up without hesitation and insisted that I keep trying. I eventually tired out before perfecting the ability, but we were all happy with the progress that I made.

The rain had gradually let up, diminishing to just a drizzle. However, the water continued to run through the parking lot as it rolled down from the nearby hills. There was no going outside today. It wasn't worth taking a chance on some object floating in the water cutting our leg. We had basic medical supplies but didn't want to risk an infection.

After dinner we played some more games. I drank some of the warm beer that I'd been eyeballing for a few days as the girls split another bottle of wine. Alexa kept her portions smaller than the night before and didn't get drunk this time. I often placed my arm around her shoulders, and she responded by placing her dainty hand on my thigh. We kissed a few times but I could tell that Jada was getting annoyed.

"What I wouldn't give for a nice soft sofa," Jada announced.

"Yes!" Alexa agreed. "Oh my God! That would be awesome. We need to get one after it dries up outside. Mason? Please!"

"Let's grab one that is big enough for all three of us," Jada added. With that she slid her bare foot up my shin under the table. She avoided looking at me as she ran her toes up and down the back of my calf muscle. Perhaps she thought that Alexa wouldn't know what she was doing if there weren't any visible clues. The contact was very sensual, and I debated on what to do about it.

"Jada," Alexa said quietly. "I know you want my man."

"Dear, if I wanted your man, I..."

"You can't hide your feelings from me," Alexa stated simply. She didn't appear to be overly angry. It was more like she was addressing a business matter with a coworker.

"That's not fair!" Jada raised her voice. "You can't just pop into my head anytime you want, bitch! There has got to be some boundaries." With that she removed her foot from my leg and I immediately missed it. I shouldn't have, but I did.

"Hey!" I snapped at her use of the B word.

"It's okay, Mason," Alexa waved me off. Then she spoke again to the temptress on the other side of the table. She was remaining remarkably calm under the circumstances. "I'm sorry Jada, but it's not like that. I'm not going into your head, but I also can't control what emotions that I pick up. Regarding boundaries, I agree. You should respect my relationship with Mason and stop trying to steal him from me."

"She's right," I chirped in. "We took you in. It's only right that you show appreciation by not interfering with us." I was trying to be careful with what I said. I wanted to support Alexa wholeheartedly, but I didn't want to chase off Jada. I was growing quite fond of her as well, just not near as much as I was for my slender blond girlfriend.

Jada looked angry for a little while as we sat there silently. Alexa and I both stared at her as she alternated looking back and forth between us. Eventually she relaxed and reached across the table for Alexa's hand. My girl accepted it easily as she took an expression looking much like sadness. She was no doubt reading Jada and sympathizing with her. I figured that was a very good thing for all of us.

"Dear," Jada said to Alexa, looking more vulnerable than I had ever seen her. "I don't want to steal your man. I do respect you, Alexa, very much. But it's not fair that you keep him all to yourself. I just want you to share. Every woman needs a man, whether they want to admit it or not. Believe me, I denied it for a long time. But it's not healthy. We are better off understanding our needs and finding solutions. Mason is a good, good man. There aren't many left in this world, I bet. Don't you think you could be a little more generous? Wouldn't you want the same from me if our roles were reversed?"

"Maybe," Alexa replied. "But I'm not wired that way. What exactly is it that you want? A relationship with him? Or, do you just need sex? Because you can take care of your sexual needs yourself. Maybe you should have more privacy."

"So, you want me to just fuck myself for the rest of my life? There is no substitute for real lovin', girl. Would you be satisfied with just touching yourself?"

"I don't know," Alexa answered. "I guess I'd do what I'd have to do. There is no shame in it."

"Uh," I interjected. The thought of these two beautiful women touching themselves was getting me uncontrollably horny. "Should I be here for this conversation?"

"Seriously?" Alexa turned to me. "There is no way you would want to miss this, I'm sure. I know that you are very attracted to Jada. And I know that you want to be true to me. But, admit it. You would love to have both of us for your lovers."

"That's not fair," I replied, shocked at the turn in the conversation. Jada, however, seemed to be delighted with it as she eagerly awaited my reply. "Yes, you are both drop dead gorgeous. I admit that. In fact, I have never denied that. I'm a man. I can't control certain things, you know. But Alexa, I love you and I want to make you happy. If that means keeping me to yourself, I am fully prepared to do so."

"I love you, too, Mason," Alexa replied. She was still holding Jada's hand. She reached for mine, too. "Maybe one day I will be a more generous woman. I don't know. Right now, I'm not totally secure in my relationship with you. Can we wait and see?"

I nodded. Of course, I nodded. Alexa loves me and is considering sharing me with the super-hot Jada. She just needs time. Not a single word was going to come out of my mouth. I just nodded and tried not to be too enthusiastic about it.

"Jada?" she asked. "Can you please be patient? I know that flirting is in your nature. I can't fault you for that. I think that I've been very tolerant of it so far. Will you respect me on this?"

Jada nodded, also refraining from speaking. We released hands and decided to play some more cards to take our minds off the conversation. When Jada's bare foot caressed my leg under the table again, I didn't object. I figured she was going to do what she could get away with without going far enough to get kicked out. She was hoping that Alexa would eventually agree to share her man. I had to admit that I was hoping the same. The question was, would I be able to handle them both?

CHAPTER EIGHT:

It was big, black and sticky. The thing unquestionably needed a thorough cleaning. Both girls said they would be up to the task, though, no problem. They obviously wanted it really bad. So, I agreed. The oversized leather sofa wasn't even as heavy as I originally expected. Jada and I were able to carry it the five hundred feet or so back to our place with only a couple breaks. Alexa kept watch for any possible trouble and cheered us on excitedly. Once back in the store I cut the bottom open to check for bugs and rodents. Then the girls took over with the scrubbing, etc. An hour later they were done and called me over to join them in breaking it in.

It was a beautiful sight indeed. We now have a large couch to fill the living room space and accommodate all three of us. It was complete with all the throw pillows that Alexa had previously collected. I had two sexy women posing as if a photo would be taken to sell the thing online. Jada was seated traditionally on the right side, her legs crossed as her bare feet rested on crate she decided to use as an ottoman. Then fair Alexa laid across the sofa, her head resting on the stronger woman's lap. One leg was raised up for her bare foot to rest on the back of the couch. I figured she had no idea how sexual the scene appeared to me. One of Jada's hands rested softly on Alexa's flat, exposed belly. I wasn't entirely sure what to make of the invitation.

"We're ready for you to join us," Jada announced provocatively. Alexa giggled. I walked briskly to the vacant seat awaiting me on the left. Alexa raised her other leg to allow room for me then brought them both down to rest on my lap. The bottom of her feet was more than a little dirty, but I didn't care. I massaged them and her calves as I reclined onto the cushions with a relaxing sigh.

"What do you think?" Alexa asked.

"I like them," I replied.

"Not my legs, silly. I already know that. How do you like the sofa?"

"It's nice," I replied. "It's surprisingly comfortable. You got it nice and clean, too. There is plenty of room for all three of us to enjoy it at the same time. All we need now is a working television and a video game console."

"You are on a couch with the two of us," Jada said feigning offense, "and you are thinking about video games?"

"No," I responded. "I'm actually thinking about how good I have it. A couple of weeks ago I could never have dreamed that I would be happy again."

"Well," Jada looked thoughtful. "You had Alexa, right?" Long pause with no response. "Wait a minute! You two haven't been together that long, have you? Why did you lie to me about your relationship?"

Both girls sat up and faced each other as Alexa responded. "We didn't really lie about it. We just kind of allowed you to be misled. But it was a survival tactic, you understand? We believed portraying a strong bond between us was important when meeting new people."

Jada thought about it for a while. "Yeah, I guess that makes sense. Still, though. You could have come clean about it since."

"Honestly," I added. "Our relationship is growing much faster than it would have in the old world. It's like we've been together much longer."

"I can see that because our friendship is doing the same. Without the distraction of jobs, schedules and cell phones, it's much easier to get to know each other quickly. However, there are still things I don't know about you guys. I talk all the time about my kids, and occasionally my husband. But I don't know anything about your families."

"Well," I replied with a heavy breath. It was true. We didn't really like to talk about all the people we lost. "My mom and dad were hard working people. We lived just up the road on Flannery Lane in Colesville. My dad worked for the federal government. I'm not sure exactly what his job entailed. My mom worked as a unit secretary at Suburban Hospital in Bethesda. That's where I watched them both pass away. I don't have any brothers or sisters. My parents would come out to watch me when I was involved in high school sports, like basketball and wrestling. Otherwise, they were home bodies. They had friends come over for a card game night every Wednesday. They played a team game called Column Master, and they absolutely loved it. I didn't have any uncles, aunts or cousins that lived in the area, so that's all there was to my family."

"What about your friends?" Jada asked, sincerely interested.

"I had a few buddies that I hung out and played video games online. After graduation we didn't stay extremely close, though. They moved out of town for college while I just went to Bowie."

"What about your girlfriend?" she inquired.

"I didn't have one when the comet hit. I was dating, but nothing real serious. Okay, that's enough about me. Your turn, Alexa."

"Alright," Alexa said. "I'm from Hagerstown, Maryland. It's a small town compared to DC, but we had plenty of shopping and even a night life scene. My parents still lived there with my two younger sisters, Avery and Madison. Unfortunately, none of them survived long after things went bad. I was at school in College Park at the University of Maryland when the comet hit. I stayed with my friends after classes were canceled. The last one of them died over a month ago. I've been on my own since then, until I found Mason."

"Boyfriend?" Jada asked.

"I had a couple different boyfriends since I went away to college, but they didn't last long. I was dating a guy named Ian, but we had only been on like three dates so far. He stopped answering my calls a while back, so I'm assuming he didn't make it either."

"Well, it's possible that his phone battery died, and he couldn't recharge it." I said, almost hoping that her old boyfriend did pass away. I didn't wish anyone harm, but I didn't need the competition for Alexa's affection.

"I did consider that," Alexa replied. "However, he never came to visit me even though he knew where I would be. I checked his dorm room a week after our last contact, but there was no one around that knew where he was. Even if he is still alive, and I hope his is, he'll never find me now. And I don't need him to because I have a new and better boyfriend."

I leaned over to place a kiss on Alexa's lips. I had no interest in rekindling any relationships from the past, and I was glad she felt the same. It was her and I from here on. And maybe Jada, too, depending on how that worked out. But I doubted that Jada could ever take the place in my heart that Alexa was quickly filling.

Jada's hand was still on Alexa's belly when I leaned over her. She then moved it to rest on my back until I sat back up.

"I can't wait until I get a kiss like that," Jada said slyly.

"What do you think?" I asked Alexa. She looked a little shocked. Then I said, "do you want to kiss Jada?" Both girls laughed at my joke. But the truth was, I would enjoy seeing the two of them kiss. I was never into girl on girl stuff before. However, I was in tight with both of these lovely women. If they kissed each other I believed that would certainly make progress in our three-sided relationship.

Then Jada spoke up, "You know, I think I'd do it."

"Do what?" I asked, trying to mask my enthusiasm.

"I'd kiss Alexa if she offered."

"I've never kissed a girl before," Alexa told Jada. "Have you?"

"Uhhhh, maybe once at a party way back when I was in college. It was a drinking game thing. It didn't mean anything. So, no. Not really. Would you like to kiss me?"

"I would have said no immediately before. But now, I'm not sure. I'm a little scared."

"Scared?" Jada asked. "Of me?"

"No. I'm scared of what it might mean. Or, maybe of what it might mean to you. Or, more likely, what it might mean to Mason. His heart is racing as we talk about it."

"Mason?" Jada feigned surprise effectively well. "Is the thought of us two kissing getting you horny? You dirty boy!"

"I can't help it!"

"Okay, okay," Alexa said as she sat up. "Let's stop. We're not doing it. This is getting me uncomfortable. Let's talk about something else."

We all three continued to sit on the couch, but we weren't making any body contact. Alexa wasn't even reaching for my open hand. I shouldn't have encouraged things, I guess. This might be a step backwards instead. I needed to put this behind us quickly.

"You know what we need is reading material. Some good books, some magazines. It's a shame we can't watch movies now that we have this great couch."

"I was just thinking about that," Jada replied. "Can't we get a generator or something?"

"If we searched long enough, we could find one, but we would need gas to run it. I'm not sure how much gas is still left in the pumps at the stations, if any. Siphoning from abandoned vehicles would probably be a regular thing. I think there would be some serious exposure risk trying to get gas all the time. Maybe we should find the gas before we go looking for the generator. What do you think, Alexa?"

"I don't know. You told me it was too risky when we talked about it before. Has anything changed?"

"Just the couch," I said. "Let's think about it for a day or two before we decide. Books, though, will be easy to find."

"They had a library at the church," Jada told us. "There had to be hundreds of books, and plenty of DVDs, too. So, we wouldn't have to go far for movies if that's what we decide."

"I think it should be Mason's decision," Alexa said. "He's our leader and he knows what is best for us. I'll trust his decision. In fact, that should be the case in most things."

"You don't think we should do majority rules?" Jada asked. I could tell that she wasn't the kind of woman that let her man make all the decisions. "Two out of three makes it easy. That's the American way, right?"

"Well, I'll vote with Mason every time, so that's two out of three. We might as well just let him decide."

"Yeah, I can see that happening," Jada replied a little deflated.

"I think we should discuss any important decisions together regardless," I said. I already considered myself the leader somewhat, but I wasn't in a hurry to raise up as such. "Whatever makes sense to all three of us is what I would decide anyway. If we had a disagreement where the two of you felt differently than me, I wouldn't just ignore you. We don't need to make a formal declaration that it's got to be my decision.

"I agree," Jada said.

"What if we get a fourth person?" Alexa asked. "That could happen. What if it's two versus two?"

"Well," Jada conceded. "In that case, both the new person and me should have less of a say, since this is your place and you welcomed us in. I can accept that. Mason's vote should be the tiebreaker."

"And if we get a fifth person?" Alexa asked.

"Okay, let's not get ahead of ourselves," I said. "It's just the three of us right now, and for all we know it could stay that way for a very long time. We'll talk about the gas and generator issue again tomorrow, as well as any other important decisions that need made. Now, I'm going to get cleaned up before dinner. I say we just chill out the rest of the day and come up with a new work list in the morning."

"Spoken like a true leader," Alexa whispered to Jada.

They both smiled and the conversation was over. We all three got our sponge baths and changed clothes. I rigged up a coffee table for in front of our new sofa using aluminum racks from the cooler and some plywood scrap. It would double as a large ottoman when needed. The girls worked together to make a nice dinner. I glanced over from time to time to see Jada casually touching Alexa. It was just simple things like placing her hand on the smaller girl's back or touching her arm while talking. Nothing too forward, but it was a noticeable increase of contact from the usual. I didn't know if it was just a sign of them getting closer, or if Jada was making a move on my girl.

Halfway through our meal we heard a noise that had been absent from our lives for quite some time. It was a combustion engine, probably from a truck. The sound only lasted for a few seconds, then it was gone. We all released a long breath that we didn't realize we were holding. Before we had a chance to talk about it another vehicle came through. We waited to see if it would pass through, too. It did not. This one came to a stop on the street beside the store, from the squealing noise made from the brakes. We could barely hear the engine slow to an idle. Then, voices could be made out. Human voices, of course. There were people out there.

We sat silently for a couple minutes waiting. Then, we heard another vehicle come to a stop. This one sounded like a big truck, maybe an eighteen-wheeler. We quietly made our way to the front entrance listening through the layers of debris that hid the door. There was no way we were going to go outside and reveal our presence to these intruders. We just had to hope these trucks lost interest in our region and moved on.

Then there was more shouting. They were probably just trying to communicate with each other over the engine noise. A little while later, two more trucks. I worried that perhaps if was a full fledge invasion. What would we do then? Fortunately, none of the voices came any closer to the store. We listened carefully for footsteps or any indication that they were headed our way. Nothing so far.

"There is a ladder to the roof in the back room," I whispered. "I could go up there to get a better look."

"I want to go, too," Jada replied quietly.

"Let's all go," Alexa said.

I guided the girls to the back room where the ladder led to the roof. Though I thought it would be sweet to follow them up the ladder, the view of course, I decided to go first so I could force open the roof door. The last time I went up there I had a hard time getting the hatch open. Thankfully, the rusted metal slab pushed up easily this time. I was careful not to make any noise as I rested the heavy hinged metal flap on the gravelly roof surface.

Crawling on the small white rocks that covered the large flat roof was too painful on our exposed knees. So, we had to crouch down as we headed for the side of the building closest to the intruders. We could hear more conversations among them but didn't make out enough to understand what they were saying. Though cloudy, it was still daylight enough to be spotted. We had to be very careful.

On New Hampshire Avenue, directly in front of the store, sat four vehicles. The first was a big black pickup truck that had been modified. It sat a good bit higher than normal on its bulky tires, with a loud dual exhaust. Apparently, stealth was not important when you felt you had superiority. The second vehicle was a box truck, maybe a twenty-footer, with some sort of food delivery company logo on the side. Next to it was a small flatbed truck, possibly designed for towing. Black tarps covered whatever equipment or supplies it was carrying.

The final vehicle drew our attention the most. It was another flatbed, but larger than the first one. This truck had a large metal cage chained to the top of it. Inside the cage were at least thirty scraggly looking people. They appeared to be all skanks.

"What the hell?" I whispered.

"What do they want with all those rotters?" Jada asked.

"I have no idea."

We continued to watch as several women conversed beside the vehicles. Occasionally, they pointed in different directions. Both my girls ducked down when they pointed to our store, but I stayed motionless. The good news was that they didn't see us. All the women of this caravan were wearing cargo shorts and tight t-shirts tucked in like it was their military uniform. They were of varying sizes and shapes, but all young to middle aged adults. I had seen so few elderly people or children over the last few months. I didn't know if they were more vulnerable to the viruses or just had a poorer survival chance in this new lawless world.

A male's voice then cracked over a speaker. One of the white women, built a little like Jada, raised the walkie talkie up to reply. Again, we couldn't make out the details. The scene continued pretty much the same for a while. Then a dozen more vehicles showed up, including another skank cage truck. We couldn't make out the details of the last few as they were too far down the road.

"Shit," Jada muttered. I agreed. This looked bad.

The male voice could be heard over the walkie talkie again. This time it sounded like he said, "let's move out." All the women then made their way to cabs of different trucks and one by one they headed north on the main road. We continued to observe quietly from our hiding spot as each vehicle passed by. The second to the last truck had several cages, each with a different type of animal.

"Are they starting a new post-apocalyptic zoo?" I jested. No one laughed since there could soon be a chance that one or all of us end up on those cages.

Once the complete convoy was out of view we headed back down the ladder into the security of our home. Silently we walked with our shoulders slumped straight back to the dinner table and sat down. Our cold food sat there staring at us, but we all evidently had lost our appetites.

"What does this mean for us?" Alexa asked.

"I don't know," I replied. "Hopefully they just keep going and we never see them again."

"What if they come back?" Jada asked.

"It would depend on what they do. If they are going to be patrolling this road regularly, we are bound to get spotted. It's possible that they try to recruit us. I didn't see any men, though. The main guy might not be interested in me."

"Well, I for one don't want to be recruited," Alexa said. "I'm happy with my current situation."

"Same here," Jada agreed.

"We may have to move then. Perhaps we are too close to the highway. We could try to find a place more off the beaten path."

"But we just got this place looking nice," Alexa said with obvious disappointment.

"I'm sure we could do it again at a new place," Jada replied. "Maybe even find a mansion that is already nicer than this. No offense, but this is a converted beer store. I think we could do better if we tried."

"I agree. Let's be prepared in case we need to leave in a hurry. I think we should have some travel bags ready, with food and water. Any personal items should be kept handy so we can grab them last minute. What do you think?"

Alexa nodded and squeezed my hand. I could tell that she was very sad at the prospect of being forced out of our home. This is where we met, where our relationship had developed. From the few stories that she told us, her life since the catastrophe had been awfully rough. She had narrowly avoided sexual assault a few times. I wanted very much to provide stability for her, but I was no match for the army that had just passed through our neighborhood. My special talent wouldn't help much either against those kinds of numbers.

Jada nodded as well. "I'll follow you wherever you go," she said. "You two are my family now. I'll fight to my death alongside you to protect us, if I have to."

CHAPTER NINE:

The next morning, I once again awoke with Alexa asleep in my arms. I could surely get used to this, I thought. Ever since I entered high school, I dreamed of having a beautiful girl to love. Unlike my friends, I had no legitimate interest in having sex with a bunch of strangers, romping through life carelessly. That did seem to be what most guys wanted if I believed what the TV shows and movies portrayed. Deep in my heart, though, I figured real men wanted that one special woman to have the rest of their life. Ultimately, that woman to me would be Alexa. She was my complete package. The way she had opened her heart to me, I knew that I would do whatever needed to keep her mine.

Then I started thinking about what happened the previous day. Just when we were getting comfortable, a serious new threat arrived on the scene. Hopefully, they kept heading north and never return to this area. But, if that group of people were forming a small army, who is to say that others weren't doing the same thing. Being this close to a six-lane highway could really be a mistake. In this new world, one mistake is all it took to get you killed, or worse.

When I kissed the angelic Alexa gently on the forehead, I accidentally stirred her awake. With her blue eyes peeping through the slits of her drooping eyelids she turned her head to kiss me on the lips and said sleepily, "I love you Mason."

"I love you, too, Alexa," I had no difficulty replying.

I held her close as she slowly ran her hand over my chest and firm belly. I was happy when she moved onto my broad shoulders. I had been putting on some muscle lately with all the exercise and furniture moving. She moaned into my neck as she continued to caress my bare skin. It was then my turn to moan when she moved on to the front of my shorts. I typically woke up every morning aroused, and today was no different. I rarely remembered my last dream, but it had to always be something exciting to get me this way. It was the first time that Alexa touched me there for any longer than one second. This time, she didn't just giggle and move on.

"I want to make you happy," Alexa whispered softly as she stared into my eyes.

"You do make me happy," I answered truthfully.

"That's not what I mean," she replied timidly. "I want to satisfy you. Sexually."

"I would very much like to do that for you as well, sweetheart."

"I know," she said. "I know that you would. And I really look forward to it. But, I'm not ready yet. I'm sorry."

"That's okay. We can continue to take it slow. I'll be alright."

"Even though I'm not ready, I fully realize that you are. You have been ready for some time now. But, please understand that my last sexual experience was some time ago, and it was not good."

"I'm sorry," I said. Did someone hurt my girl? "Do you want to talk about it."

"No. Maybe one day, but not today. It would ruin this morning, and I don't want your morning to be ruined. I want your morning to be wonderful. You deserve it for how well you have treated me. So, I'm not very experienced at this. You'll have to tell me what you want."

With that Alexa pulled off my shorts, then my boxers. I swiftly got over my hesitation and guided her through the process of how to work her hands effectively. Alexa's learning experience was delightful to share. Her enthusiasm for satisfying me made a huge difference and it wasn't long at all before she finished the job. There was a lot more kissing after that and swearing our love to each other. Then we scrambled to get me dressed when we heard Jada approaching.

"Good morning," Jada said from the other side of the counter. She couldn't possibly see us where we were lying. "I hope I didn't interrupt anything."

"Uh, no," I responded, zipping up my fly while standing. It was a motion that was hard to conceal.

"No, we're done," Alexa said as she leaned into to me for a warm embrace, smiling with her eyes closed.

Jada smiled a toothy grin as she glanced between us. "Well, good for you," she said, no malice in her tone. "I just wanted to say good morning before I started working out. I have a tendency to have a narrow focus I get once I get a sweat going. Let me know if you need any help with breakfast, Alexa. You know I'm happy to do anything you two lovebirds need."

"Thank you," Alexa replied. "I'll be fine. I'll join you this afternoon for exercise, if you don't mind. I'm a little tired this morning."

"You are welcome whenever you want, dear. You know that. Mason must have given you a work out already this morning."

"Sort of," Alexa replied, her beautiful face beaming as she walked over to the kitchen area, a little bounce in her step. Even though our sexual interaction was completely one-sided, the way she enjoyed it said a lot to me about her unselfish personality.

Jada took a quick look at my tented shorts and pushed her tongue against the inside of her mouth. She then turned away heading for her space on the far side of the store. Over her shoulder she said, "You are welcome to join me too, Mason."

I watched her sexiness saunter away from me. This time I was not inclined to follow. My affection for Alexa was at an all time high.

"I want to scout the area from the rooftop first," I said. "If everything is clear, I might get in a quick morning workout."

"We should work on honing your deflection skills some more. Practice makes perfect," Jada said.

I was extra cautious moving around on the roof just in case, but there was no one nearby from the recent convoy of trucks. There were, however, several small groups of the zombie like people hanging around. Three skanks were sitting up against the wall outside of the church next door where we had met Jada. It was as if they were waiting for someone to let them in for religious services. I got the feeling that maybe there were much more inside the building. The notion of searching over there for books might be a very bad idea. I'll have to warn my roommates.

To the south I saw a few deer grazing in one of the yards with tall unburnt grass. They weren't frothing at the mouth or chasing around other animals, so I assume they were surviving normal, just like me, sort of. A lone scroungy looking dog meandered his way down Hollywood Avenue away from me, stumbling from time to time. His condition could be due to disease or hunger. I couldn't quite tell from this distance.

Far to the north on New Hampshire Avenue, heading toward Colesville, were some trucks in the middle of the road. I could barely make out their forms in the early morning fog. I couldn't recall if they had been there all along. It could be the group of militia girls from yesterday or abandoned vehicles from months ago.

What I really needed was a set of binoculars. Did I see some in any of the houses that I raided? I couldn't remember.

I didn't tell the girls what I had seen. No sense worrying them unnecessarily. Instead, I said that there were a few small things I was going to look for in nearby houses. I made up a supply list to make it look legit, stuff like tape, cable ties, knives, and the like. As I was clearing my exit Jada came up behind me dressed in her usual tight outfit.

"I'm going, too," she said. "I want to find some paint."

"I can look for it," I replied.

"No, that's okay, I might find some other stuff I need while I'm there."

"I'm not comfortable leaving Alexa alone," I said, prepared to hold my ground on the matter.

"Oh, she'll be fine."

"Lexie!" I called out. I had only used the pet name a couple times so far. "Will you be okay alone for fifteen to thirty minutes? Jada wants to search for some stuff as well."

"You're leaving me here by myself?"

"Not if you aren't okay with it," I replied.

"You'll be fine, Lexie," Jada said, making fun. "I'll be back in just a few minutes myself. I only need a couple things and I'll probably find them in the first house or two."

"Okay," Alexa replied hesitantly.

I wanted to continue to object, but it seemed like the matter had been settled. We barricaded the front entrance even more securely than usual after exiting, then headed to the first house on our street. It had been picked over a few times already, but just for basic needs. Now we were looking for specific non-essential items. Once inside Jada headed for the basement and I looked for storage space on the top two floors. I found a few things on my list, but no binoculars. As I approached the basement door, I heard Jada call out below.

"Hey, Mason! I think there is something down that here you want."

I trotted quickly down the steps to see what she was talking about. I figured the bottom level of the house might be the best place to find the remaining things I needed anyway. I came screeching to a halt as soon as I left the bottom step, though. Jada was standing there in front of me completely naked. Well, except for the sneakers. The concrete floor was dirty, so that was understandable. The nakedness was not.

Jada's body was absolutely amazing! Every muscle was tight, but not bulky. Her medium brown skin was so smooth, and there didn't appear to be a strand of hair anywhere below her neck. She had been keeping herself groomed like an exotic dancer. Apparently, she applied lotion like one as well. I was mesmerized by the incredible sight as she began to walk toward me seductively. I knew I should turn and run, demand that she put her clothes back on, but I was thoroughly entranced by the provocative scene.

"Mason, I'm sure that I can take care of your sexual needs better than Alexa," she spoke softly as she slithered closer. "I'm not asking to take her place in your heart. I know you are a loyal man, and that is one of the many things that I like about you. I'm just proposing that we handle certain matters on the side."

I still couldn't move when she reached me, pressing her firm body against mine. I felt her large globular breasts push against my abdomen as she looked up into my eyes like a temptress. I couldn't help but allow her to guide my hands to her tight round ass as she kissed me softly on the chest through my t-shirt. Her hands then began to roam my body in search of muscle and my arousal. Guiding one of my hands to her breast she stood up on her tip toes to plant a soft kiss on my lips. My thumb brushed gently across her large dark nipple as our tongues eventually found each other. When I pulled my mouth away to gasp for air, Jada smoothly squatted down in front of me and began rubbing her nose against the firm protrusion in the front of my shorts. Her gorgeous brown eyes and sexy smile when she looked up at me could have made her some serious cash as a photo online back in the day. I knew that oral sex from this woman squatting in front of me would likely be the best sexual experience of my life. My body was eager for her attention.

Then Jada stood up and took a step backwards. I thought maybe that it was my turn to make an advance toward her. I hesitated, of course. I tried desperately to get my brain to overpower my testosterone. I needed to snap out of this daze she had me in. I already had a great thing going with Alexa. Likely, our relationship would continue to grow to be everything I always wanted. I would be an idiot to blow it. Thankfully, Jada spoke.

"So, that's just a small taste of what you can expect if you take me up on my offer. I know that you don't want to leave your girlfriend alone too long. Did you find everything you were looking for?" With that she started gathering up her clothes off the laundry table and began getting dressed. I remained motionless watching her as she did.

"Mason?" she smiled at me. "Are you going to be okay?"

"Yes," I stuttered. "Sorry, uh no, I didn't find everything yet. I want to search the basement before moving on to the next house. You're right. I don't want to leave Alexa alone. She'll probably be safe, but I don't want her to worry about me."

"Oh, I bet she is worrying about you alright. Because you are alone with me."

"Obviously, she has reason to worry."

"Do me a favor, Mason. Honestly, I don't want to break you two up. I am happy to be a part of your group and I very much want to stay there. Please don't tell Alexa about our brief encounter. Nothing really happened anyway. There is no reason for you to feel guilty. If you decide that you aren't interested in my affection I will back off and you won't have to worry about me again."

"Well, you just gave me reason to worry about myself."

"No," Jada said firmly. "That's not being fair to yourself. I was seducing you. It's not your fault that I'm so good at it."

Now that she was completely dressed and my body was returning to normal, I decided to forget about the near sexual experience and return to my search. I was lucky to find a small pair of binoculars in a storage cabinet, so I didn't bother to continue searching for the other items on my list. Jada gathered up a few things, too. It would appear to Alexa like we found everything that we were looking for, so we headed back hastily.

Alexa was indeed worried, as I expected. After greeting her and stowing my stuff I went straight to the roof explaining that I would like to test out the newly acquired binoculars. They both wanted to join me, but I told them that I wanted to be alone for a little while. That was probably not the best choice of words. I could clearly see that Alexa was immediately suspicious of our friend, but I left before anything more was said. The colorful flashes on her face were brief but plentiful.

Once I made it to the north side of the roof, I no longer gave any thought concerning what to do about Jada. The trucks up the highway unfortunately looked to be part of the military girl convoy. Additional bad news, they appeared to be setting up a barricade across the wide road to block unwanted traffic. I couldn't tell if they just intended on controlling New Hampshire Avenue, or if it was the first step in setting up camp in the area. The magnified lenses helped me figure out what was up there, but not enough to alleviate my concern.

I needed to consider doing some recon. I didn't want to take the girls if I did, but I also didn't want to leave them alone. What if I get caught and never return? In that case, I would need Jada to take care of Alexa for me. It was important that I help solidify their friendship. This sexual advance of Jada's wasn't going to help in that endeavor. I decided not to tell Alexa about what happened in the basement. At least, not just yet. I had to put the safety of our trio before anything else.

As I headed back down the ladder, I could hear shouting in the main room. The girls were arguing. My desire to improve the bond between them would now need a lot of extra work. This fire needed put out first, though. Did Alexa sense what had happened between Jada and I while we were gone? Did Jada break down and tell her? What was I heading into as I rejoined them in the store that had become our home? They were both standing there in the living room area as they pointed and yelled at each other, close enough for a physical altercation. The conversation that I heard since closing the roof hatch had not been pleasant.

"You fucking whore!" I heard Alexa say. I had never heard her so angry before.

"Whoa, bitch!" Jada answered back fiercely. "Don't you ever call me a whore!"

"Or what? You'll beat the shit out of me!"

"No!" Jada said. Then a little calmer. "No, Alexa. I would never hurt you, though we both know I could."

"Just not physically," Alexa added. "You don't give a shit about me emotionally then."

"I'm sorry," Jada said, more heartfelt than I expected after the heated exchange.

"What's going on?" I asked.

Alexa turned to face me, turning one leg sideways and placing her hand on her hips. I expected her to start tapping her toe on the concrete floor like a mother impatiently waiting for her child to get in line.

"Is there something you want to tell me?" Alexa asked.

I glanced between the two girls. Without any skill like Alexa's special ability I couldn't be sure how much information had been shared between them. I was in a tight spot. I decided to use my limited talent to deflect the situation.

"Yes," I replied as I stared at her. "Two things. First, I love you always and forever, and I will never betray you." Alexa softened a little as her face flashed blue. "Second, the caravan that headed through here yesterday is setting up a barricade on the main road just to the north. They may be here to stay. So, whatever issues you two have with each other right now, I suggest you put them aside as we figure out what we want to do."

CHAPTER TEN:

We were still a couple blocks away from the newly erected street barricade when we could hear the truck engines idling. Sound traveled much farther in this quieter, less populated new world. Regrettably, I couldn't convince either Alexa or Jada to let me scout the precarious situation alone. Being responsible for the safety of all three of us made the recon mission that much harder for me, and slower. Truth was, Jada looked like she could handle herself alright. And Alexa was good enough at hiding. However, neither of them observed their surroundings well enough in my opinion before popping out from cover. Alexa also had an aversion to crawling. Oh, she would do it if her life depended on it. You would just have to convince her that it did. She did so few things to annoy me, but that was one of them. I did my best to be patient in that regard.

While hiding behind a short faded white fence with large green trash cans, we watched as three of the army girls corralled two skanks. All three girls were black and athletic, but not as attractive as Jada. It was Alexa that pointed out that fact. The two skanks were in surprisingly decent shape. If they had been standing still at a distance, I could have confused them for regular people. Their clothes weren't any more torn up more than had once been the style. One of the girls had an open wound on her arm, though. And the other had a limp that suggested an injury under her jeans that refused to heal.

The tormentors used long poles with padded hooks to snag their captives. Once they had them contained the tallest girl spoke into her walkie talkie, "We have two more rottens, both bitches of course. Do you want them in the cage?"

"Are they in good enough shape to work?" another woman's voice cracked over the speaker.

"Yeah, these are better than average." The woman on the other end of the line said to cage them up. We watched as the militia girls used wooden clubs along with their specialized snares to guide them up the street. They were noticeably avoiding physical contact with their rotting flesh. Though we couldn't make out all the words used by the skanks it sounded like they were having a conversation with the girls. Perhaps they were asking where they were being taken. They weren't being treated overly rough considering. It's possible that captivity would be a better life for them, I considered. Maybe they were being well fed and given shelter in exchange for decent work. It didn't seem likely, but it was possible. I had always been prone to optimism in the past. It had been much more strenuous to maintain that outlook since the fall of society. But my limited association of late had me rebounding to happier thoughts.

Once the coast was clear we retreated three houses east, away from the main road before moving one more block to the north. It wasn't long before we encountered another capture. Only this time they already had the guy in custody. He was a light skinned man, a little smaller than me, not quite as buff, wearing jean shorts and an unbuttoned vertically striped shirt. His black sneakers looked practically new. His arms were behind his back, no doubt bound securely. But that's all I could really make out, since they had a black hood over his head.

The man's body had a variety of cuts and scrapes. His capture may have been necessarily more violent than the skanks. I could hear his rough voice complain about the heat of the hood, begging the five army girls there to pull it off.

"No way, Jose," one of them replied. "We ain't taking a chance on you flashing us those sparkly emerald eyes. Just stay put until Moe gets here. He'll know what to do with you."

Apparently, this guy had mutated green eyes like the wolf that mesmerized the skanks a few days ago. That time when we were trapped in that house with our wagon on the porch. He must be able to put people in a trance by just looking at them. Reluctance to remove the hood was understandable.

"We ought to just kill these mutants," another one said. "I don't see why we take a chance. You remember what that sparker did to Latisha? Nope, that ain't gonna happen be me."

"It's Moe's call," the first one answered.

"I think those sneakers might fit me," another of the girls said, causing the whole group to laugh.

I wished there was something I could do to help the poor guy. I considered the possibility of rescuing him, but all five girls held rifles or handguns. Even if I could dodge a thousand bullets, I wasn't willing to take a chance on Alexa or Jada getting shot. The best chance would be getting the guy's hood off so he could keep at least keep some of them from shooting in the first place. Both my girls were dead set against that plan, even though Alexa could feel his fear and sorrow. Before I could come up with a more desirable proposal, several more of the militaristic people showed up. I assumed the lone male was Moe. He dismissed the original five girls causing them to go back on a search through the neighborhood. That was bad news. We had to go.

We darted back the way we came before any of them headed our way. It took us a while, mostly due to my extreme caution, to arrive back at our place. Luckily, the store was undisturbed and free of intruders nearby. Once back inside we all sat at the table to discuss what we had seen and possible actions we could take. We were all softhearted toward those that had been caught. But we believed it more important for us to avoid the same fate ourselves than try to rescue them. When Jada went for her afternoon workout Alexa and I remained at the table to talk more privately.

"How can she think about exercise at a time like this?" Alexa asked.

"I think that's how she deals with stress," I answered.

"I'm scared," Alexa said.

"I know. I am, too."

"No," she said. "Not like that. I mean, I'm worried about what is happening out there on the streets, but I'm confident that you will get us through it. What I'm talking about is being scared of losing you to Jada."

"I already swore that I wouldn't let that happen."

"I know, I know," she replied. "But I can tell how attracted you are to her, and I can't blame you. The woman is smoking hot. Her confidence in her abilities assures me that she would be a much better lover than me. I'm scared that I can't compete with her."

"You don't have to compete with her."

"Eventually I will. If the three of us stay together, you two will end up having sex. It's inevitable. I've almost come to terms with it. But not only will she want sex more than I will, she'll also be a lot better at it. No matter how much love you have in your heart for me, I will lose you to her if I don't make some changes."

"What kind of changes," I asked instead of challenging her assumptions.

"I'll have to get a lot better at sex, for one thing. Getting comfortable making love again after all this time will be essential. And, I have to be first."

"What do you mean first?"

"I need to make love to you before she does. If I'm second, I'll lose you. I know it."

"No, I..."

"Stop, Mason. I know that you believe that you will be able to control yourself. But when you can't, you will blame yourself. And I will blame Jada. Then our relationship will be a mess. I desperately want to avoid that. So, I say that we should make love tonight. And soon again after that. Let me get my confidence up before we allow anything else to happen."

"I can't say that I agree with everything that you have said, but I am definitely looking forward to tonight. Love you Lexie," I said, then kissed her on the forward before leaving the table.

"Love you, too, Mason."

Alexa then started working on what we should have for dinner while I went topside for another look around. Things were pretty much the same at that point. There were a few skanks hanging around the church still. I remember the militia girls calling them "rottens." So, they also understood that these weaker individuals were not zombies. It probably wouldn't be long before they decide to raid that sanctuary and take captive any of them that could be put to work.

I joined Jada for some exercise and made a concerted effort to avoid checking out her body as she moved through various work out positions. The physical activity pumped blood through my brain. It also helped me think clearer about our possible options for dealing with the current crisis.

When I started tiring out, I announced that I was ready for more deflection practice. Jada had used the paint that she acquired earlier to make some targets on the wall. I worked on tossing various projectiles into the air, then sending them at the bullseye. My aim and velocity were steadily improving. I continued to practice when Jada went to get cleaned up for dinner.

A few minutes later the dark-skinned beauty reentered the main room wearing a casual dress that caught me totally by surprise. It wasn't as tight as her normal attire but showed some cleavage and only dropped down to mid-thigh. The flowery pattern did not seem like her style to me, but none of us had an extensive or selective wardrobe these days. This garment had been taken from the house where we had been trapped for s short time by the wild dogs versus skanks experience.

Draped over Jada's arm was another dress. This one was light blue. I watched as she completely ignored my uncontrollable stare and headed for the kitchen area. The sight of her in the dress was nice, but I had just seen her completely naked earlier in the day. Perhaps the sexy woman would not be as distracting since that encounter. I had hoped, but here I was with my tongue practically hanging out of my mouth.

I paused my routine of kinetically shooting debris at the wall so I could clearly see what Jada was going to do. The girls talked quietly so I couldn't overhear most of the words. I didn't need to, though. I watched as Jada displayed herself for Alexa to see. My girlfriend obviously complimented her sufficiently. Then Jada showed Alexa the dress that she picked out for her. My girl was apparently very pleased. They talked some more, some of it looking to be quite serious. There may have been an apology on both sides. And there were probably some tears based on their sad expressions. Then they hugged each other. The embrace lasted a long time, like when my mother used to comfort me as a child. When they finally broke it up, they continued to hold each other at arms-length to communicate some more. A little while later came another embrace.

I stood there observing the whole scene like it was an emotional moment in my favorite television show. The two characters that I cared most about were pouring their hearts out. Only I couldn't hear the words. I was essentially watching a silent movie, trying not to miss any nuance.

The second hug didn't last as long, but they didn't pull away when it was done. It looked like Jada wanted to hold Alexa close. Then it happened. She kissed my girlfriend on the lips. I was surprised, but not as aroused as I expected to be. The smooch was not the passionate kiss that I may have been fantasizing about. It was a gentle peck, followed by eye contact, resembling something you might give a family member in an emotional time.

When Jada turned to leave, Alexa pivoted my way to see me watching. She smiled and waved, holding the blue dress with one hand and wiping tears from her eyes with the other. I waved back and she laughed. Surprisingly, Jada didn't look my way at all. She went straight to where we kept the dishes and began setting the table for dinner. In the process she grabbed two bottles of wine that Alexa had set aside earlier. Then she added a six pack of wheat beer that had become my preferred brew for consumption at room temperature. I wondered if the day would ever come when I could once again drink a nice cold beer.

After I got myself cleaned up, I took over kitchen duties which were at the point of transporting the food to the table. Then, Alexa went to get bathed and dressed. No doubt she was going to put on the dress that Jada had picked out for her. I looked forward to seeing her in it. I myself, did not have anything fancy to wear, but I did put on a clean buttoned-down shirt. It was a little tight in the shoulders, but it would be adequate for dining. I wasn't going dancing or shooting pool.

"So, what was all that about?" I asked Jada as we eventually waited at the table for our third member to arrive. She knew that I was talking about the emotional exchange between the two of them in the kitchen. We were seated in our normal arrangement. The table had two chairs on each side and I typically sat on one side with Alexa, facing Jada directly across from me.

"Girl talk," she answered simply.

"That's it?" I asked. "I believe I saw some hugs, maybe a few tears. And was there a kiss?"

"Enjoy that, did you?"

"Truthfully," I replied. "I enjoyed watching you two get along. And, by the way, you look very nice in your dress."

"Thank you, Mason. You are very handsome in that shirt. And thank you for shaving. Neither Alexa or I were fond of the that scruffy beard that you had started."

"Scruffy?"

"Yes, scruffy."

Then Alexa entered the room. Oh my God. I didn't think the slender blue-eyed blond could look any more beautiful. I was wrong. The simple light blue dress didn't fit her perfectly, but it was a delightful change from her normal more casual attire. She wore no jewelry. In the old world I would have vowed to change that, get her a nice necklace and earrings to accent the look. A glittery pair of sandals did adorn her tiny feet. There was no polish on her toes, or fingernails for that matter. Still, she was quite a sight. Her long blond hair was pulled back with some kind of clip that kept the sides of her lovely face exposed while sheeting her straight hair down the back.

"Alexa," I said as I approached her, nearly knocking over my chair. I could see how much she was seeking approval in my eyes. Her face briefly flashed blue as she picked up my emotions unnaturally. I knew that she couldn't help it. The extra sense was simply a part of who she was. Of course, I had nothing to hide. "You look stunning."

"Really?" she asked sincerely, even though she knew how I felt. Her lack of confidence simply kept her from quickly accepting the compliment.

I pulled her close and planted a passionate kiss on her lips. It was more than you would normally do in front of others, but not enough to get her to wrap her leg around me. I fully expected Jada to tell us to get a room, but she enduringly stayed quiet during the exchange. I held Alexa back enough to get another look at her. The dress hung straight down, not accentuating her curves sufficiently in my opinion. It ended about mid-calf on her cleanly shaved smooth legs. The neckline was too high to show any cleavage from her modest breasts, but I could clearly see her nipples poking against the soft fabric. She obviously was not wearing a bra. I couldn't make out any panty lines, either, though that was harder to tell. The thought of her naked body under the thin blue material was getting me very excited for what to expect later.

Instead of following me to her customary chair, Alexa went around to the other side of the table to hug Jada once again. Our friend complimented her appearance as well, then they both sat down for dinner. The mood was great as we forgot about our worries for a while. We pretended like we were all out at a fancy restaurant, taking turns describing our preferences.

Jada longed for a penthouse patio view of the city, with all the lights of activity glittering in the darkness. We would all be in formal wear, deck out with fine jewelry.

Violins playing in the background, the chime of champagne glasses being tapped gently together. Then she said we would systematically view everyone in the fancy restaurant one table at a time and guess what they were there celebrating.

Alexa preferred a beach deck with umbrellas protecting her delicate skin from the blistering sun. Calypso music played in the background with steel drums. Her sandals on the floor beneath a counter height table as her sandy toes rested on a rung of my chair. She wanted wide glass cocktails with their own little umbrellas, and appetizers with toothpicks in them. The sound of the waves would roll in as we reminisced about our experiences together. She made a point of saying that I would be shirtless, it was a beach bar after all. Jada made a fake coughing sound instead of verbally announcing her agreement with that part of the scenario.

When it was my turn, I told them that any restaurant would be fine with me, as long as I was with the two of them. When they forced me to choose, I described a castle setting in the mountains overlooking green hills with a dark blue sea in the distance. Bagpipes would play as we all three danced like gypsies and sipped disgusting mead from wooden cups. Though neither of them fancied my choice, they enjoyed envisioning the scene that I painted for them.

I managed to drink all six beers over the course of about three hours, as we sat and talked about our favorite vacation spots after dinner. I had a good buzz going on, but I was far from drunk. Jada drank most of the bottle of red wine and was getting a little wild, but Alexa went easy on the blush beverage. I caught her glancing my way each time she took a tiny sip. I believed she was determined to stay focused for our evening rendezvous between the sheets. I was grateful.

After cleaning the table, we decided it was time for all of us to go to bed instead of playing card games like we had earlier considered. Before Jada headed to her section, she gave us each a firm hug and a kiss on the lips. "You two have fun," she said as she walked away. I began to wonder if Alexa had shared her plans for tonight. After Jada's kiss, which was just a brief reminder of our moment of almost passion in the house next door, I glanced at Alexa to get her reaction. Happily, she just laughed and shook her head.

Earlier in the day I had installed a curtain rod system around our sleeping area for privacy. If we stayed there in the old beer store, we'd eventually have to get nicer curtains than the green tarps I currently had hanging from the metal poles. Once behind the barrier I pulled Alexa close to my body and kissed her, softly at first. Then, each kiss became longer and more passionate until we found ourselves melting onto the sheets below. I caressed her shapely body all over as we continued to explore each other's mouths. My gentle hands found her firm modest breasts. She did not resist, so I explored lower to grip her ass, pulling her against me. Again, she responded favorably. This was going to happen. Finally.

"Take it off," she whispered into my ear. Assuming she was referring to her dress I eagerly obliged. I pulled it carefully over her head to expose her nude form with all the appropriate areas cleanly shaved. I was so excited to begin kissing her body that I didn't even remove any of my clothes. She lied there groaning as I kissed and licked her body all over, quickly bringing her to a climax that had her screaming profanity. Though a little shocking, I thoroughly enjoyed her display of extreme pleasure. Instead of worrying about the noise drawing attention from people outside the building, I expected Jada to show up to see if her friend was okay. Thankfully, the other woman left us alone, though it was possible that she was on the other side of the tarps listening to the whole thing. I didn't care. I was enjoying my time with the love of my life, and nothing was going to interrupt us.

As Alexa recovered from her orgasm, I removed my clothes. When she made like she was going to return the favor, I pulled her mouth back up to mine. "I need to..." she said into my mouth as she tugged on my erection. "No, you don't," I replied. "Not this time." I lowered her onto her back and continued to kiss her softly on her neck and face. I guided her as best as I could through a traditional sexual experience that had her moaning and screaming two more times before I couldn't go any more.

She quickly fell asleep in my arms, exhausted. I watched her angelic face as each slight glimmer of blue on her skin was followed by a smile. I was not an experienced lover by any means. However, my growing affection for Alexa, and deep desire to please her had served me well, I thought. I was worried before that the sexual experience would remind her of some bad instance in her past. Instead, she gave herself over to my control without hesitation. I was more than happy with the results. I was also glad that she could now have the confidence associated with successful love-making. I got the distinct impression that she was worried whether or not I would enjoy it. All things considered it was possibly the best experience of my life. And I would never forget it.

CHAPTER ELEVEN:

I spent a half hour after breakfast the next day scouting meticulously from the roof. I had to be careful not to be spotted as I unhurriedly rotated from side to the side, making notes of everything I saw. I was disappointed in myself that I had not been doing this all along. I could see surprisingly well from my perch on a sunny day with the use of the binoculars. I vowed to never go without this advantage ever again.

The church next door was now a hub of skanky activity with rotters coming and going regularly. So far, the militia girls had not found them. There was still one truck parked by the barricade way up on the main road to the north, but most of them had moved on. Maybe they had taken all the recruits that they needed for now.

A good distance to the south, just on this side of a major intersection with exit ramps, sat another barricade with a similar truck. I had not seen that before. Apparently, they were planning to take control of the area by blocking the major routes. I could see from my weathered road map that the side streets on both sides of the main road eventually led to neighborhoods. Those then connected to Randolph Road to the east and the west. That meant that people could take these streets to avoid the main road. However, to the southwest, there were several roads that didn't go anywhere. If I wanted the best privacy, that is where I should be. The tall trees down that direction blocked the entire view, though. If I wanted to scout it, I would have to do it on foot.

Jada and Alexa were exercising when I went roof side, with plans to do some weapons training. When I eventually returned, they were instead engaged in a heated battle of the Castles & Catapults card game. Alexa had seven gold played to Jada's one, evidently stealing most of it from her opponent. Once the game ended, I shared with them my idea of scouting the neighborhood to the southwest. My intention was to find a more secluded place to live. Both girls hated to leave the store that had become our home but agreed that we were way too exposed to any groups passing through. After a quick lunch all three of us were packed and ready to go.

We carried our backpacks loaded with supplies to last us a couple days, just in case. And some weapons, too. Jada had her spear, hatchet, and two sheathed knives. I brought knives that I kept in a pouch hanging from my belt, and a bag of marbles for use with my ability. Alexa brought the baseball bat and a pocket knife. She wasn't comfortable yet with any exposed blades. We didn't plan on bringing back any new supplies, so we wouldn't have to bother with the wagon slowing us down.

We stealthily crossed the main road by the store onto Norcross Way, which I had scavenged before. Ignoring the houses there, we made our way through the properties of three more churches cautiously. I saw a few skanks wandering around all of them. Were they drawn to the religious aspect of the facility or just the size and shape of the building? If ever people were likely to find religion, it was when they were at their lowest. You couldn't get much lower than a skank, I'd think.

All the recon and sneaking around to avoid detection made the journey time consuming. We had traveled less than a mile in two hours when we came across a high school on Valley Brook Road. Though it was off the beaten path, the size of the complex would draw too much attention to be our new home, I thought. And all those entrances? That would be a real challenge to defend. It looked like the best path to the next street would be right beside the school. As we approached the building, I could see movement near the front entrance. There were two girls there with hunting rifles. The variety of cars parked in front of the education facility were regular sedans, no cargo or transport trucks in sight. This was likely a different group than the one blockading New Hampshire Avenue.

The three of us stayed hidden in the woods at the edge of the soccer field for several minutes as we observed the school grounds. There were another two girls with rifles that appeared to be on patrol, circling the pale brick building. Each woman that we had seen thus far were not wearing anything that resembled a uniform. I figured that they might be more of the survivalist type than military. They did not carry themselves like soldiers.

Just the same, we took a wide path around the school as we headed over to the next couple roads. Houses there were well spaced apart, and of decent size. With so much open space between them, it took us forever just to check out just a few houses. Some had been broken into and well picked through, but there were a couple that seemed like they might make good new homes for us. We started a list of potential locations making note of all the pros and cons to each.

At the end of Warrenton Road, we came across a river and a long driveway leading to four more houses up a hill according to the mailboxes at the entrance. Since you couldn't get much more remote that that, we decided to check it out. About halfway up the driveway we spotted two more of the rifle toting women headed our way. They were involved in a conversation, too distracted to spot us. Quickly, we darted into the thick brush beside the narrow asphalt passage and waited. The movement had evidently caught their eye and they were approaching our location cautiously.

"Alexa? Can you sense anything?" I asked.

"Yeah, a little," she replied quietly. "They are nervous, but not scared. I don't think they consider us a serious threat at this point. Maybe they are not sure what they saw."

"They might think we are skanks," Jada said. "We could use that to our advantage."

"I think you are right," I replied. "Why don't you try to circle around behind them. Don't get caught. We'll be too far away to help each other. I'll stay here and protect Alexa. When they get close, I might have to show myself. Watch for my cues."

With that Jada worked her way silently through the underbrush behind us to get some space between her and the driveway before heading up the hill. I lost sight of her quickly, which meant she was successful in her stealth. Hopefully, there weren't more of these rifle women wandering around. So far, they always seemed to be in pairs.

We waited patiently for them to get close to our position. Before they reached an angle to see Alexa cowered down behind a stump, I decided to reveal myself. I was prepared to dodge bullets, if needed. My heart was racing at the idea, not fully confident in my abilities yet. I wanted to try the diplomatic approach first. That would also allow Jada more time to flank them.

"Hello!" I said loudly as I stepped from the woods onto the pavement with my hands visible. They were maybe thirty feet away from me still. "I mean no harm. As you can see, I don't have a gun."

"Who are you?" the first woman asked. I guessed that she was in her thirties, dirty blond hair, a little stocky. Her brunette partner might have only been just a teenager from her appearance. She was a plain looking thin girl wearing boots that were clearly not made for hiking. She in particular looked worried when I stepped out of the woods. They were not expecting to find a healthy man, no doubt. The two rifle barrels were raised in my direction hastily. I began to wonder if I could dodge two bullets at the same time.

"My name is Mason."

"Who are you with?" the blond asked taking a protective stance slightly ahead of the younger girl.

"Nobody. I'm alone."

"Hah," the woman replied. "No real man is alone in this world. Are you sick?"

"No, just hungry. Do you have any food you can spare?"

"We have food back in our compound. Put your hands on your head and turn to face downhill. We'll take you there and let Mac decide if you are worth feeding."

"I'm no threat to you or your people," I replied. I did not want to put myself in a blind position by following her orders. Hopefully, Jada was already in position. I couldn't see her. "If you don't have food to share just let me go. I'll find my own somewhere else."

"No, you won't," the older woman responded. I could see now that the teenage girl was scared outright. She was almost trembling with her finger on the trigger of her small rifle. "We'll shoot you where you stand before we let you go."

That's when a familiar spear came flying out of the brush just twenty feet away from our opponents to strike the teenager in the back of her thigh. She screamed out, of course, and fired a shot in reaction to the blow that nearly grazed me. The older blond turned quickly and fired a shot toward my warrior friend who was now exposed along the roadside, her hatchet in her hand. I focused hard on deflecting the shot from hitting Jada.

She must have been confident that I would do just that. Instead of diving for cover she threw the hatchet to strike the woman directly in the face. I cringed immediately from the gruesome sight. My guess was that she died instantly as she fell backwards to the ground with her rifle still clutched in her hands.

The brunette girl was already on her ass trying to pull the spear from her thigh. As I approached, she snagged up her rifle quickly and fired a shot at me. Just ten feet away I ducked as I deflected the bullet, just in case. I could see Jada running up with a long knife in her hand like she was prepared to decapitate the girl.

"No!" Alexa shouted as she left the cover of the stump. Obviously, she was feeling the girl's fear and became sympathetic. I could understand that, but now I had to protect Alexa from getting shot.

The brunette turned to fire her weapon at Alexa, but nothing happened when she pulled the trigger. While she cocked the weapon to load another round, I picked up a hefty rock from my kneeling position and tossed it in her direction. Using my special skill, I adjusted the aim to strike the rifle and knock it out of her hands. It worked wonderfully. Now that our foe was weaponless, Jada's knife blade stopped just short of the girl's exposed neck. My friend looked like a super sexy female version of Rambo.

"Don't kill her!" Alexa shouted.

"She'll report on us if we let her go! We don't need a bunch of armed enemies searching for us." As Jada replied she looked straight at me instead of Alexa. She was awaiting my order.

"I won't tell!" the girl cried out, trembling with tears pouring down her freckled face. How could I order the death of a defenseless young girl? Now that we were up close, I guessed her to be just fourteen or fifteen years old.

Jada noticed the expression on my face and knew that I didn't want the girl dead. She slowly withdrew her blade and picked up the girl's rifle instead. I stepped closer and knelt before our defeated enemy as I tried to figure out what to do. Was there a risk to letting her go, like Jada suggested? She didn't seem like much of a threat. Maybe she joined this clan against her will. Perhaps she would be better off joining us.

"Are you a captive of your people?" I asked.

"No," she sobbed. "I joined them with my mother. We don't really take prisoners."

"Is that your mother?" I asked, gesturing to the assuredly dead woman with the bloody face on the ground beside us?" She shook her head. "Is your mom still alive?" She nodded. "What will you tell them if I let you go?"

"I'll tell them that we were attacked by a pack of wild dogs and I got separated from Ashley. It has happened before. I'll say that I don't know what happened to her. They won't know that you killed her until they find the body. No one will come this way until they do patrol tomorrow."

"How far do you patrol?"

"From this road up to Meadowood," she answered. "We stay away from the main road, too."

"Mason," Jada said. "Can we take that chance that she won't tell? Even her story could have them searching for this woman tonight."

"I promise!" the girl cried out. "I'll tell them we got separated closer to the school where we stay. I don't care where you people go. We just want to protect ourselves and our territory. They won't find you unless you stay here. I promise."

"Alexa?" I asked our truth finding member. When she nodded, I knew it meant that we should let her go.

"Let's bandage her leg," I said.

"Thank you," the girl sobbed, crying even more now that she knew she was going to live through this. I really felt for her and was tempted to convince her to come with us. However, having a family member still alive in this world was so rare, I couldn't consider separating them. She was best off staying with her mother even if their circumstances were not ideal.

"We're going to move Ashley's body off the road, so she won't be found easily," I told the girl. "I'm sorry that we killed her."

"I understand," the girl said as she began to regain her composure. "We were going to shoot you. Sometimes it is kill or get killed out here. I don't like it, but what can I do?"

"You didn't like her, did you?" Alexa asked the girl.

The young lady shrugged her shoulders and said, "She wasn't the nicest person in our clan, but I wouldn't wish her dead. No one will be terribly upset that she's gone."

The brunette then limped down the driveway hastily without turning back. Once she was out of view, we continued up the hill to check out the four houses anyway. If this was the edge of their colony, and they truly were not looking to expand, we could possibly make this area work for us. It was so remote that I didn't want to cross it off the list without checking it first. After that, the new plan was to go east toward the main road and then head home, taking note of the area we passed through as we went. I didn't want to linger very close this group's territory longer than necessary without a good reason.

Jada retrieved and cleaned her weapons. Sometimes she seemed so hardcore that I wondered for a brief moment if I had misjudged her personality at all. If I didn't know her better, I would assume she was a natural born killer by her behavior during a crisis. Truth was, though, that she had just successfully come to terms with what she needed to do to survive in this world. I was a little envious of her for that. It seemed like we made a good threesome. I tried to be realistic but compassionate when I could. Jada was willing to do whatever it took. And Alexa, mostly due to her gift perhaps, was sympathetic with everyone. Together we could make the best decisions.

We were a little tired after the long hike up the hill and were glad when the first house finally came into view. We gave it a quick once over before moving on to the next, eager to be done with it. The broken windows and debris in the front yard, combined with the small size of the building, made it less desirable than other houses already on our list.

Alexa's extra sense came in quite handy when approaching each building, or new area for that matter. She could easily tell if the building was occupied by picking up their emotions, possibly even while they were sleeping. Leaning on her helped us move quicker than my customary cautious approach.

It was all a matter of routine by the time we jimmied open the front door of the last house. That one was nice and tidy except for a few bags on the kitchen counter. Perhaps someone had stayed there for a while recently. Jada checked the bags and declared that they were indeed survival supplies. I glanced at Alexa again to verify that we were alone. She shook her head, so I decided to check the bedrooms for anything that might tell us more.

I opened the first door on the right, which turned out to be a bathroom. Pulling that door closed I moved on to the next. Before I could get that one all the way open, I was struck in the forehead with a wooden baseball bat. I didn't see it coming in time to deflect it. The person attacking me must have swung the thing with all their might. I knew nothing but the pain it caused at that moment. I felt my eyes cross as I lost clear vision and fell to the floor in front of a small pair of women's sandals, which were occupied by thin, pale skinned feet. Then everything went blank.

When I finally woke up, I was seated on the sofa in the living room of the same house. I had obviously been placed there after I passed out. When I tried to lean forward my head throbbed with excruciating pain. I attempted to pull both hands to my face, but one was gripped by someone else. I turned to see Alexa's beautiful face smiling at me.

"Mason, you're awake. Thank God, I was so worried about you." I complained about my headache when she pulled me into a hug, but I was delighted that she was okay. Things could have been much worse. Without my protection she might have been killed or taken captive. I still had no idea what was going on.

I could hear two female voices in the kitchen. One was Jada's, but I didn't recognize the other. It was high pitched and soft at the same time, like something delicate and musical.

"He's awake, Jada," Alexa announced after kissing my cheek.

"Oh, good!" Jada replied as she hurried into the living room. "I told you he was a tough one. Here's a wet rag to hold against your head, dear. We don't have any ice, of course. How are you feeling?"

"Just a bad headache," I said.

"Are you nauseous?" she asked as she placed her face so close in front of me that we could kiss. At first, I thought that was her attention. Instead, she glanced between my eyes possibly checking for dilation. I had just entered into concussion protocol.

"No, I don't think so."

When Jada pulled back, I could see the other girl enter the room. I looked to see if her feet were touching the ground because she appeared to glide toward me so smoothly. There I saw the sandals from just before I passed out. The young woman was extremely thin, possibly twenty pounds lighter than Alexa, with pitch black hair and pale skin. Her eye color was so dark that it seemed to match the blackness of her pupils, making deep mesmerizing pools on a perfectly angelic round face.

She stopped short, a little hesitant and spoke as if singing a hymn, "Hi Mason, it's nice to meet you. Jada has already told me so much about you. I'm so very sorry that I hit you with the bat."

"That was you?" I asked rhetorically. I recognized the sandals. Now to put the pieces of this puzzle together. How could this have happened?

"She caught you off guard, didn't she?" Jada smirked.

"Yeah, especially since Alexa didn't sense anyone in the house."

"I still can't sense anything from her," Alexa announced. "She must be immune to my gift."

"I'm Riley, by the way," the girl said with a timid smile, then reached forward to shake hands now that she could see that I was not overly angry. Her skinny long fingers barely gripped mine as she allowed me to simply shake her seemingly fragile hand. When I released it, her fingertips seemed to linger on my palm as she pulled away. Combined with her angelic appearance the effect was a little intoxicating. It was hard to believe that she was actually the person that knocked me out.

"Do you remember when I told you about Riley?" Jada asked. Yes, of course, this was the girl that Jada ran with before they got separated. We would never have found her if I hadn't decided to search this neighborhood.

Alexa cleared her throat to get my attention. I had been caught staring at the new girl. Though not nearly as sexy as Alexa or Jada, she had a way about her that made her very attractive, somewhere between an elf queen and the good witch of the north.

"So, Mason," Alexa said coyly. "I think the answer is obvious, but I have to ask. Would you like Riley to join our group?"

CHAPTER TWELVE:

"Sure," I replied guardedly, somehow making it sound like I had more to say. The dainty girl looked like she surely needed protection, if I could quickly forget her ability to swing a baseball bat at someone's head. Then again, she did catch me by surprise. I should have been more alert and not relied so heavily on Alexa's gift.

Riley's immunity to my girlfriend's sensing ability wouldn't be of much help against others, unless of course she was immune to all special gifts. But how would that work? Some abilities were more physical in nature.

I realized then that everyone was still waiting on me to continue. "I mean, if it's alright with you two. She's a friend of Jada, right?"

"Sort of," Jada replied. "We didn't get to know each other well, but I'm all for adding her to the group."

"Alexa?"

"I'll go along with whatever you decide, Mason."

"Do you have any concerns?" I asked my girlfriend.

"Not really. It's just kind of weird that I can't pick up on what she is feeling. But in a way, it's kind of nice."

"Riley, have you been on your own since you and Jada were separated?" I asked. It would be good to know now if anyone would be looking for her.

"Yes, sir," she answered respectfully.

"You don't have to call me sir. And please take a seat while we talk."

"Okay. Thank you. Jada told me already that you don't rule your clan as strict as the other men. But as the new girl I wanted you to know that I will always show you respect, especially since Jada is so fond of you. I mean as a leader."

"Yes, Jada is very fond of my boyfriend," Alexa added under her breath.

"Well then welcome to our little group," I said to the thin black-haired girl. "You referred to it as a clan. How many of these clans have you encountered?"

"Oh, maybe a dozen or so."

"How many members are in each clan?"

"That can vary greatly. A good leader will draw more girls to him and win even more from battles with the other clans. There are some men, too, that will join the bigger clans. Most of them are weaker, though. I was in a couple clans already, and they both had over twenty girls. The clan that defeated my last one must have had at least fifty, though. That was the biggest one that I've heard about."

"Are there many groups as small as us?"

"Not so much in the city since they get taken easily by bigger groups. Yours is the smallest faction that I have met so far, but I'm betting that it will continue to grow nicely under your command."

Riley's mild manner combined with her ultra-respectful behavior made her very easy to like. She was also the only girl that I've come across in months that was wearing a dress. The thin, dark green fabric floated in the air as she moved and glided smoothly across her body when she crossed her legs. Those pale thin limbs lacked the muscle tone that I was typically drawn to, but for some reason I continued to look.

"If I may be so forward," Riley said, lowering her gaze. I could tell that she wanted to approach a subject that made her slightly uncomfortable. "Jada tells me nice things about you, but I would like to know from you first hand regarding your, um, how do I say, your sexual policy."

"My what?"

Jada interjected, "I believe what Riley wants to know is if she will be required to sleep with you. I told her that you weren't like that, but she'd be more comfortable hearing it from you."

"Oh, no. Of course not. Do the clan leaders you know all rape their women?"

"Yes, sir. I mean, it's not really raping since the women agree to the terms when they join the group. Though, there are some clans that take captives for that purpose. I shudder to think what they have to go through."

"Would you like to have sex with my boyfriend?" Alexa asked, obviously annoyed by the subject. She had become more forward with this girl since she couldn't get a supernatural reading on her. Jada laughed.

"No, miss Alexa. That's what I'm trying to say. I will follow all your rules, of course. But I would prefer not to take a turn in Mason's bed, if that is allowed."

"Well that's good to hear," Alexa said. "That's all I need is more competition. But, just to be clear, if sex were required would you still join us?"

"Wait a minute," I interrupted. "That's inappropriate. You don't have to answer that, Riley."

"It's okay," Riley replied. "I know that Alexa is your top girl and I should answer any questions that she has. I understand that she is especially concerned about me because of my immunity to her gift."

"I'm liking you more and more by the minute," Alexa stated.

"The answer to your question is yes. If Mason required sex from me in return for his protection, I would give it to him. That's the way the world is now. I would need to join a clan eventually. Your man seems like the most respectable leader I have met so far. To be honest, this is a great opportunity for me."

"Well I'm glad that he isn't like that then," Alexa said sourly.

"Miss Alexa, I would even have sex with you if Mason required it. I'm not like that by nature, though. I mean, I have never been attracted to girls. In fact, I'm not really a very sexual person at all. But I want to secure my place here with you. If either you or Mason demanded it right now, make no mistake, I would crawl over and satisfy you orally as best that I could."

"Whoa!" Alexa responded in shock. "That won't be necessary, though I'm betting that Mason would like to watch that."

"Me, too," Jada said, adjusting herself in her seat.

"Mason?" Riley asked me, seemingly emotionless, waiting for my command to have her lick my girlfriend between the legs. For an instance I visualized the fantasy. It would be something that I might like to see. My hesitation to respond earned me a slap on the leg from Alexa.

"Mason!" she said blushing, pulling her legs tighter together instinctively. "Stop it!"

"I'm sorry," I finally answered. "No, Riley, that won't be necessary. But thank you. Now, I think that we should get ready to go home. I'd like to get out of this clan's territory soon, and back to our place before dark."

I told Riley that we can help carry any stuff that she wanted to take with us, but we might need to ditch some things if we had to run. Her cache of supplies was not extensive. She was very appreciative of the offer and willing to do whatever I asked of her. I already believed that she would be a valuable addition to our team.

As Jada scouted ahead and Alexa focused on sensing any enemies nearby, I had more time to talk with the pale skinned waif. "So, Riley, do you have a special gift like Alexa? Or is immunity your new talent."

"I believe I do have something. I was not aware of the immunity gift before today. However, I acquired something special a couple weeks ago. For one second, I can move at an accelerated speed. That was how I was able to strike you with the bat in the house. For that again I am very sorry."

"Oh, okay," I responded. "I feel a little better about it now. I was wondering how a little girl like you, no offense, was able to knock me out."

"No offense taken," Riley replied. "I think my little girl appearance, as you call it, helps me catch people off guard. It does make me tired, though. If I need to use my ability two or three times within a few minutes, I would need to sit down and rest for a while. The same is true if I stretch the length of the burst. I guess that it is a recharge of sorts."

"Still, that is an awesome talent," I said. "I'm sure it can give you quite an advantage in combat."

"It is yours now."

"Excuse me?"

"My talent is yours to use as you wish. I will trust that you will not abuse it or put me in a position of higher risk than necessary. I will only use it when you command, or when I feel it is absolutely required to assist the clan in a crisis."

I didn't have time to respond as Alexa stopped abruptly and grabbed my arm. Her expression of fear and alarm had me concerned. "Alexa?"

"Jada is scared!" she said. "She's around the corner of that house, and I can't sense anyone else there. I believe she is standing still."

"Well, let's go see what it is," I said as I ran forward. Riley joined me, still able to glide as she sprinted. She was more graceful than a gazelle. I wondered if she was like that back before the world went to shit.

"Be careful, Mason," Alexa called out, not keeping up with us due to the fear she was sensing from Jada.

The problem became obvious as soon as we rounded the corner. A lone wolf with pitch black hide and green eyes stood before Jada. He had been slowly approaching her until we were spotted. Jada didn't even have a weapon raised. She must have been mesmerized by that emerald gaze. Then the beast stared right at me and I felt it, too. I couldn't move. I was still able to see clearly what was going on, and fear that I was going to be eaten by the wolf, but I could not do anything about it. Not a muscle in my body responded to my command.

"Oh shit!" Alexa muttered when she caught up. Then the wild dog stared at her, also. This beast must have been more powerful than others we have seen if it could affect multiple people at the same time. It glanced between us every so often to continue the influence.

The three of us stood there paralyzed as our newest member took quick action. She slowly lifted the wooden bat that she used to clobber me earlier that day and took a deep breath. When the wolf turned to her she bolted forward at incredible speed and whacked that fucker in the head before he could dodge the blow. A yelp erupted from the thing briefly, then it fell to the ground, presumably dead. Instantly, the three of us were released from its spell. Fortunately for everybody, Riley was immune to the animal's trance.

"Oh my God!" Jada yelled out. "I thought I was going to die! Thank you, Riley."

Jada went quickly to Riley and hugged her. The thin girl responded with less enthusiasm for the embrace and replied, "You are welcome, Jada." I could see that the new girl was feeling tired from her exertion, but Jada didn't notice.

"Riley, I am so glad you joined us," Jada continued. "Feel free to use any of my stuff. Hell, you can even share my bed. By the way, will you also take orders from me?"

Riley turned to me expecting me to answer. Apparently, she would sleep with Jada if I commanded it. And Jada almost seemed to want it. Damn! I am liking this new girl.

"Jada!" Alexa shouted. "Stop being so horny all the time and leave Riley alone. She is not our sex slave. Thank you, Riley for saving us. Don't let Jada make you do anything you don't want to do. Understand?"

"Yes, thank you. I am so glad that I was able to be of value to the clan so quickly. I'm kind of exhausted all the sudden, though." Jada and Alexa helped Riley lower herself to the ground to rest.

"How long does it take for you to get your energy back?" I asked.

"A few minutes," Riley answered like she was drifting off to sleep.

"We don't have a few minutes," Alexa said. "I think there are some people following us. They must have heard horny Jada screaming out."

"Oops, sorry," Jada said as she readied her spear looking back the way we had come. "How many of them?"

"Maybe four," Alexa responded as she focused her skill.

"Are they the rifle girls?" I asked.

"I don't know."

"Okay, this is what we are going to do," I told them. "We've got to keep moving. Jada and Alexa, take the bags that Riley was carrying."

"I don't think she can walk, Mason," Jada objected.

"She won't have to. I'm going to carry her until she gets her strength back. Let's go."

We never did see who was following us, but Alexa kept us posted on their distance. They matched our pace until we reached New Hampshire Avenue. Once we crossed, they turned around and left us be. At that point Riley was back to her normal self which made it easier for us to cross the main road quickly and unseen. The sun was setting behind us in an orange glow as we made our way through the barricade back into the old beer store that we called home.

I was more than a little tired myself by the time we all got inside. It had been a very eventful and stressful day. We encountered more enemies with rifles. Jada injured one and then killed another. I got whacked unconscious with a baseball bat. We gained a new member to our team and she saved us from a trance wolf. Then, I carried her in my arms for almost ten minutes as we hurried home while being followed by unknown predators. I'd had enough excitement to last me a while.

Riley wasn't awfully heavy, but it was a little awkward carrying a virtually limp adult while jogging. She kept her arms loosely around my neck as I cradled her in my arms. Her dress rode up as we bounced which placed her creamy thin thighs against my skin. I was distracted by it at times but tried not to think too much about it. Her beautiful face and large dark eyes were even a bigger problem. Occasionally, I saw Alexa glancing at me perplexed.

"I'm sorry," I told my girlfriend once Riley was able to walk.

"I know," she responded, then leaned in for a quick hug. It was tough having my emotions read all the time by my lover, but at least she was understanding. Given a choice, I wondered if most women wouldn't prefer to have that knowledge. Some of it might be shocking at first, but then once they realized that we had nothing to hide, it might be for the best. I couldn't say for sure. Understanding one woman was difficult enough for me. Trying to understand them all would be impossible.

Though Riley's emotions were not all that evident, I could tell that she was delighted to be joining us in our home. She was surprised at first to learn that we had chosen a retail store for our domicile. She said some clans were based in shopping centers with furniture stores. Most took over apartment buildings to gain the comforts of home while limiting access to the building. It made a lot of sense to me. If we had to end up moving, we should consider that.

Riley eagerly assisted Alexa in making a quick dinner. We were all starving from the long day. Jada and I moved some shelving to form a bedroom for our newest member, then gathered some blankets to provide cushioning for her bed. After the meal the girls insisted on teaching Riley how to play Castles & Catapults. They were so excited to have a new player. I took the opportunity to go topside and look around again. It was a clear night, so the moonlight provided some visibility. There wasn't much to see, though. That was good news. Maybe we had some time to rest before figuring out what we wanted to do.

When I came back down the three attractive girls were all on the couch telling stories. I approached slowly trying to eavesdrop, just for fun. Alexa knew I was there, of course. It was good to hear them laughing with each other. There wasn't much to laugh about in this dystopian society. It was the first time I saw Riley truly smile. It was a very nice sight indeed.

"You three having fun?" I asked as I walked up. There was no room left on the sofa for me, but that was fine. It was just about bedtime. They all answered to the affirmative. Then I asked Riley, "Are all the clans enjoying themselves like this?"

"No, Mason," Riley answered with her elegant soft voice. "You have the happiest and most beautiful women by far."

The comment felt so good that I almost cried. I quickly composed myself to make sure I didn't tear up, but it was too late. Alexa jumped off the couch and gave me a necessary hug. She continued to cling to me in comfort, something I rarely needed. At that instant I knew that I truly loved her and would do anything for her. With my eyes closed enjoying the moment I didn't see Jada coming to join in. We welcomed her into the threesome embrace, of course.

After a few wonderful seconds Alexa called for Riley come, too. Jada and Alexa parted to allow Riley in, wrapping her into the circle with their arms when she pressed her tiny body against ours. I hated to break up the embrace, but I suggested that we all get some much-needed rest.

"May I give Mason a kiss goodnight?" Jada asked Alexa.

Alexa smiled and answered without much hesitation, "Sure."

The gorgeous dark and sexy woman grabbed my face with both hands and kissed me square on the lips. It was brief but meaningful. I expected Alexa to complain. Instead she asked Riley if she wanted to kiss me goodnight as well.

"If it pleases you miss Alexa, I would be happy to," Riley answered.

Alexa nodded, so Riley stepped forward and placed the softest kiss ever on the tip of my lips. We almost didn't touch, I thought, but my lips tingled as evidence that we did. She then nodded slightly as she backed away before turning and following Jada to their side of the store. I stared after her in wonderment at the experience.

"Are you okay?" Alexa asked.

I laughed and said, "She is a very unusual woman." Then I gave my girl the best kiss I had in me attempting to take her breath away. When I released the lip-lock I gallantly scooped her up in my arms and carried her off to bed.

CHAPTER THIRTEEN:

The next morning, I woke to Alexa's hot breath and velvety kisses on my belly. Once she noticed that I was awake she began to tug off my shorts. I didn't complain. As usual I was already physically prepared to receive some sexual attention. My girl might have been timid and inexperienced, but she was determined to satisfy her man. I only gave instruction when it was asked for, but plenty of moaning feedback when she was doing well. And I thought she was doing quite well. The sight of my beautiful mate's face being using to bring me such pleasure was positively amazing, despite her laid-back technique. I don't know how far I was supposed to let her go because I wasn't sure if she was going eventually mount me or complete the task orally. She stayed vigilant with the fellatio and followed through with passion. She was profoundly delighted when she finished the job to my satisfaction. Her vocal celebration from bringing me to orgasm was louder than any noise that I had made during the ordeal, and I thought I was being too loud.

"You didn't have to finish me off like that," I whispered heavily as I tried to catch my breath. "You know I love to bring you pleasure."

"I know," she replied softly. "I'm okay. I really enjoyed doing this for you this time."

"Is everybody okay over there?" I heard Jada yell from her side of the big retail space.

"Yes, thanks for asking," Alexa hollered back joyously. "We're doing great!"

"Sounds like it," Jada answered, not quite as loud.

As we were getting cleaned up, we heard the undesirable sound of trucks outside once again. I quickly scurried to the roof with my trusty binoculars. In the broad daylight of a cloudless morning I knew that I would need to stay very stealthy. I instructed the girls to stay below and remain as quiet as possible.

After gaining a westward viewpoint close to a large post for cover, I slowly popped up just enough to see with my naked eye. There were four trucks visible on the main road adjacent to the church parking lot. That was uncomfortably close to us. I could see that some of the militia girls were already actively rounding up many of the rancid folks that were hanging around the church grounds. There were no shots fired yet, but some of the armed women were getting a little rough with the weaker diseased people. Then a man hurriedly stepped out of the truck and told them to go easy. He was an older guy, slightly bald, wearing something like a linen suit. Healthy men were very rare to see these days. Someone wearing long pants and a jacket were even rarer still.

"They injure easily," he explained in anger. "Don't be any rougher than necessary. We need them at their best."

It seemed like their entire focus at this point was on the area around the church. No one appeared to be searching farther into the neighborhood from what I could see. Two of the trucks had pulled into the parking lot to have supplies unloaded and taken inside the building. They had apparently decided to make it a base of operations for this section of their domain. That was extremely bad news for us. I had to tell the girls right away. When I turned around, I almost let out a yelp of surprise to see Jada's gorgeous face right behind me. She had obviously refused to follow my instructions to stay below. At least she was being careful not to get spotted, crouching slightly lower than me.

"Damn it, Jada," I whispered. "What are you doing up here?"

"I wanted to see what was going on. The girls are worried downstairs and I didn't know how long you would be up here observing. What can I tell them so far?"

"Oh, okay," I said. That would allow me to stay up top a little longer while Jada passed them some details. "Well, the militia girls and trucks are back, and they are taking over your church. They're clearing out the skanks and have taken captive the decent ones, just like we had seen before. Tell Alexa and Riley to start packing. We might have to leave soon before they come looking around over here."

"You don't think we should stay and fight? Do we have a chance? Our collective abilities and the element of surprise could outweigh their numbers."

"Not a good enough chance to get all of us out of it alive. It's not worth it. We should just move," I said.

I turned back to the edge of the building and started using my binoculars again. I didn't hear Jada leave behind me, so I looked back her way. She hadn't moved an inch. Instead she was checking out my body. I had time to put on my shorts before I heard the trucks but went shirtless to get up to the roof as fast as I could.

"What are you doing?" I asked impatiently.

"I'm just looking," she said as she rested her hand on my bicep. "Did you have a good time with your girl this morning?"

"Jada, now is not the time. Please go back down and get them started packing."

This time she did as she was told, but not without a couple backward glances and a sultry smile. The woman was so sexy and seductive that it was hard to be upset with her bad timing. We should have been in crisis mode, not flirting. Her hormones must have been in high gear that morning. The sound of Alexa and I having some intimate fun probably made it worse.

I continued to watch the group unload supplies and set up a perimeter of guards around the building. So far, they were not leaving the church grounds. That gave us some time, but how much? It was hard to say. I tried to read lips with the magnified lenses, but I couldn't make out anything useful. At one point it looked like the older man told a younger rifle toting girl that he liked her tits.

But I could be wrong. I was not very skilled out making out the words at a distance. The next sentence that I thought I could lip read was "grab your heart and get to boogie." I finally gave up and went below.

"How much stuff should we take?" Alexa asked in near panic.

"As much as we can carry. Just prioritize. All the essentials first, then lots of water, then some food. We don't know where we'll end up." All three heard my instructions and nodded. Thankfully, Jada appeared to be much more focused on the task at hand than previously.

We barricaded the front entrance after we all exited, hoping to hide our existing living quarters for as long as possible. We preferred that they not come searching after us. There was not enough time to toss the store well enough to completely cover our trail.

We then set out due south at first, away from the church, going as quick as we could without abandoning all caution. A few blocks away we paused for a quick break.

"There aren't many skanks about," Jada said. It was true. They had either all been rounded up, killed, or scared off. I hadn't seen one yet since we left the store.

"What is a skank?" Riley asked. We all chuckled at the question. It sounded so funny coming from her soft melodic voice.

"That's what we call the female people that can't heal. The guys we call skunks, but there aren't near as many of them, of course." Alexa was the first to give the explanation.

"Oh," Riley responded. "Everyone else is calling them zombies. I know that is inaccurate, because they are not the living dead, but that's the term that is popular. However, I must say, I like the skanks and skunks option much better."

"Me, too," Jada said. "I used to call them zombies and didn't think twice about killing them. Appreciating that they are still alive has kind of changed my viewpoint."

"Okay," I interrupted. "Once everyone has enough to drink, we should continue to head away from the intruders. We will also cross the main road at some point and then get as far away from it as possible. We have two destination options the way I see it. I'd like to get your opinions before we decide where to go."

"Really?" Riley asked with perplexed expression.

"Sure," I replied.

"It's going to take you a while to get used to Mason, I think," Jada said to Riley.

"I look forward to it," Riley answered her.

"First option," I told my girls, "is to find a nice big house that we can take over. It will already be furnished, so that would make it better than the store. There are plenty of them off the beaten path, so we'll be secluded. However, if someone stumbles across us, we might have trouble defending the place."

"I miss our sofa already," Jada said, trying to lighten up the moment. "I think the big house sounds like a good idea."

"Me, too," Alexa added.

"Wait a minute," I said. "Listen to option two. We could take over a small apartment building instead. It would also be furnished, possibly with big sofas. The advantages of that option would be better security and privacy. There would be limited access that we could fortify. It would be easier to defend than a house. And, each of you could get your own apartment."

"Wouldn't you and I be staying together?" Alexa asked, sounding hurt.

"Yeah, sure," I answered. "That's not what I meant. I was saying each of you women could have your own place."

"Then Mason can take turns where he sleeps," Jada offered seductively. "I'm fine with waiting my turn. It sure as hell would be more than I'm getting right now."

"No," I said annoyed. "That's not it either. Damn it, Jada. Can we have a conversation without you bringing up sex?"

"It's okay," Alexa interjected, touching my arm. "She didn't mean any harm."

"Thank you," Jada said to Alexa.

"Alright, how do you all feel about it?" I asked.

"I vote for the house," Alexa said. "I like seeing us as one family, having dinners together, playing cards in the evening, and helping each other every day."

"I agree," Jada said. "The privacy of our own apartment would be nice in some ways, but I would definitely miss being around you guys every day."

"We can still have a common space where we gather, or visit each other's apartments," I said.

"It wouldn't be the same," Alexa and Jada said together.

"What about you, Riley? What do you think?" I asked.

"I'm fine with whatever you decide, sir. I mean Mason."

"No, Riley. I'd like to know how you feel about it before I decide. You are part of our group now. You get a voice. You earned your spot yesterday, for sure."

"Well," she hesitated. "Initially, I would have promoted the apartment building idea. That's what I have seen done successfully by the other groups. However, you guys are not like the other clans. That is crystal clear already. Your friendship is very strong. I can see that easily. And, I must admit, I'm a little jealous. I have not really had a friend since mine all died from the viruses. I can visualize myself holed up in my apartment and not joining in activities unless you asked. The idea of us all four together every day is very appealing to me. The experience I had with you all last night was one of my favorite moments in my life. So, I vote for the house, too, if I get a voice."

"Wow," Jada said, placing her hand on Riley's arm. "You really opened up."

"Yes. It's not something I do often. In fact, it has been a while. I'm not used to being asked my opinion. Did I say too much?"

"No," I responded first, and reached for her dainty hand. Again, her soft touch and angelic face were mesmerizing. "I truly appreciate you sharing your feelings. The fact is, I was leaning toward the apartment building idea myself, for security reasons. But with all three of you expressing your desire to stay like a family unit, I must agree. I want the house, too. Let's go find one."

The farther we got from New Hampshire Avenue, the more distanced the houses were. However, we did see a few more skanks than earlier, and a lot more animals. Now that we had four in our group, perhaps we would be much less likely to face an attack. When it came to crazed beasts, though, anything could happen. We continued to use the extreme caution that I stressed with my girls daily.

Eventually, we ended up on Apple Grove Road. It held the last wooded neighborhood going south toward the city before things got more urban. The houses there weren't as large as the ones on Warrenton. But that is where the rifle girls were patrolling when we had that altercation that cost a woman her life. I would just as soon avoid them.

We were well into the afternoon searching the variety of houses. The buildings that were suitable for us, and not already busted up, were just a few. We made our notes and figured we would check out a few more before deciding on one. They each had features that the girls liked. It would take a little work to get them fortified to my liking, though. Too many of the properties had been heavily vandalized or had animal carcasses or human corpses that would need attention. Yuck. It would be easier to just pick one that was reasonably clean already.

Then we hit the gold mine. As we approached, I could tell that it was a huge single floor white brick home with a shitload of solar panels on the roof. If I could figure out how they worked, we just might be able to have some electricity. Also, all the doors and windows appeared to be unbroken. The security system was extensive, but no longer active. There was a four-car attached garage with its doors closed. If there were cars in there, we could find a way to move them out and possibly use that space for something. The tennis court and swimming pool in the back yard wouldn't likely have any realistic function, though.

We were all excited to check out the inside. It did not disappoint. A large open living room with a three-hundred-and-sixty-degree fireplace won the girls over immediately. Though it was always too hot to need one. The kitchen was fancy and included a ten-foot by three-foot marble-top island. Five bedrooms! That left us space for guests, if we ever had any. The basement was absolutely wonderful, too. A game room complete with pool table, foosball table, and six player poker table. There was a large bar down there already well stocked with liquor and wine. But, my favorite aspect of this house was the workshop that was below the garage. It was full of lumber that could be used to board up all the windows and secure the doors. We could make this awesome place even more fortified than the beer store. I was sold, and so were the girls. Alexa ripped up our notes on the other houses to solidify the decision.

The long day had taken its toll on us. We were all utterly exhausted. The brown leather sectional on one side of the living room had seating for four, plus the corner piece. We all crashed there for a while trying to regain our energy. There was a minimum amount of work that would be needed before we could safely sleep there that night.

Riley sat properly upright on one end, her legs crossed, and her hands folded in her lap. Alexa laid her head on the arm cushion of the opposite end and stretched her shapely slender body across two seats. They were seated before me. I, of course, decided to sit beside my girl, lifting her feet to rest on my lap. I felt like laying down, too, but resisted the temptation. It would only make me more tired. I still had work to do.

Jada continued to walk around a little, not yet done talking about how much she loved the place. So, she was the last to take a seat. Perhaps it had be her plan to be. Instead of taking the open seat by Riley, she plopped into the corner section. It wasn't long before she laid her legs across the vacant chair and her head beside my lap, propped up on her arm.

"Your feet are dirty," she told Alexa. It wasn't an insult. It was just something to say since her face was just inches from said feet.

"I did a lot of walking today in sandals," Alexa replied, completely not offended by her friend's remark as she wiggled her toes.

"They stink, too," Jada said with an ornery smile.

"Hey, they do not!" Alexa replied, faking hurt feelings.

"Alexa's feet are precious," I jumped into the conversation grabbing my girlfriend's feet.

"They are?" Jada asked. "What other parts of Alexa do you think are precious?"

"I love all her parts."

"Such as?"

"What are you doing, Jada?" Alexa asked.

"I'm just curious what Mason's favorite parts of your body are."

"Well," Alexa replied before I could. "I know he likes my legs. He touches them a lot. And my butt. He also kisses my belly a lot, so I guess that's one of his favorite parts."

"Anything else, Mason?" Jada asked. She was determined to get herself and others horny this evening, that was for sure. Riley just watched silently with mild amusement.

"If you must know," I replied. "I like everything about her physically. Her face, her eyes, her hair. I like her slender arms and legs, and that tight little butt she mentioned. I adore her breasts, and her other private areas, too."

"Do you now?" Jada replied as she rolled up off the sectional sofa to stand directly in front of me. "What about my body?"

"Jada," I said. "I can't..."

"It's okay," Alexa said. "Go ahead. Tell her."

"I.... think this might be a trick," I answered.

"No, it's not," Alexa smiled at me without budging from her reclined position. Judging by her tone and body language I had no reason to debate. It just didn't sound like a good idea. I waited, but Alexa didn't say anything else. She just smiled.

"Well?" Jada asked impatiently. Apparently, she had no intention of backing down from this situation.

"Okay," I finally said, reluctantly. "I like your dark skin. It's very smooth looking. I also like your muscular arms and legs. They aren't too big to take away from your natural attractiveness." I turned to see Alexa looking at Jada instead of me. I figured that was a good sign.

Jada turned around and poked her butt in my direction. "Do I have a nice ass?"

"Yes, Jada," I answered begrudgingly. Alexa laughed. "You have a nice ass."

Then Jada turned to face me again and pushed her breasts together, bouncing them around a little. "How about my titties?" Now Alexa and Riley were both laughing outright.

"Yes, Jada. You have nice big breasts, as well."

"What about my face and my hair?"

"You are beautiful, Jada," I answered. "I think that you already know that. And I think you already know that I find you attractive. What are you doing? This isn't going to end well, I think. We were just so happy to find this place. Please don't ruin the evening."

"It's okay, Mason," Alexa interjected. "Jada? Would you like to sit on Mason's lap?"

"Whoa!" I said.

"Yes," Jada answered eagerly. "Would that be okay with you, Alexa?"

Alexa nodded. Her smile never faded, so I wasn't sure how much I should resist. She seemed to be treating it like a game. But I was sure that someone was going to end up getting hurt. Before I could object Jada straddled me instead of sitting across my lap. She slid forward to push her knees deep into the sofa, her butt resting on my upper thighs. This was too much, I thought. I could feel myself getting aroused already.

"Kiss her," Alexa called out.

Before I could say anything in response, Jada grabbed my face in her hands like she did the evening before and placed a big wet kiss on my lips. She pulled back just enough to look at my reaction, then Alexa's. My girlfriend was still acting as if all this was okay. So, Jada kissed me again, this time more passionately. Without my brain registering what my body was doing, I slid my hands up her firm thighs to find her tight round butt. Then she kissed me one more time before I came to my senses and pushed her back. I was losing control, with Jada, right in front of my girlfriend. This was terrible, I thought.

The milk chocolate skinned beauty was obviously enjoying herself. My hormones screamed out that I was, too. This time when I looked at Alexa she appeared to be in shock. Her eyes were wide, and her jaw dropped.

"I'm sorry," I said instinctively, even though it was clear to me that this development was not my fault. I knew this was going to happen. Why did I let it?

I could see Jada returning to her senses as well when she looked at Alexa, who had become her best friend these days. Without me having to demand it, Jada slid off me to stand up. I was full on excited, my pants tenting for everyone to see. And all three of them looked. Then Jada laughed.

What happened next, I could not have predicted. Jada fluidly took the same position on top of Alexa, straddling her as she was reclined sideways on the sofa. My girlfriend tried to object, but Jada started kissing her playfully on her forehead and cheeks. Eventually the fairer skin young woman below her started to giggle.

"Stop!" Alexa said, though it looked to me like she was not seriously complaining. But Jada did eventually cease the barrage of affection.

"Give me one good one on the lips, then I'll leave you both alone," Jada said.

"What? Why do you want to kiss me?" Alexa asked.

"Because you are beautiful, Alexa. And you just let me kiss your man. I would very much like to show you my appreciation. Then you can take Mason to bed and do whatever it is you two do, this time behind closed doors."

Alexa continued to giggle until Jada turned more serious, playing with my girlfriend's hair. She then brushed her finger across her lips. Then Alexa whispered, "okay, but no tongue." Jada slowly descended toward Alexa's mouth. I leaned forward to get a better look in my excitement. While I observed naughtily, Jada gave her a long and sexy kiss, lasting a little longer than I had thought Alexa would allow. It was Jada that ended it before she had to be pushed away. When she dismounted my woman, she gently patted the front of my shorts before she walked bewitchingly away from us.

"Alexa," she said over her shoulder. "You need to take care of Mason's needs now. I'm going to bed. And I need some private time for sure."

"I still have work to do," I told the girls, wishing I could immediately follow Jada's suggestion as well.

"I'll take care of securing the doors for the night," Riley said as she stood up. "Don't worry, Mason. I'll stay on watch until you are rested. Go spend some time with your top girl."

Alexa already had me by the hand and was leading me to the bedroom that we had selected as ours. Thank goodness we had already put on a clean sheet earlier. We were both ready to go at it. It was a very active sexual experience for us this time, not slow and easy as our previous times. We were both satisfied quickly in our passion for each other. The encounter was much more animalistic than I thought either of us would have chosen. But somehow, it was just right at the time.

We plopped onto the mattress on our backs to catch our breath. After laying her silky blond head on my bare chest, Alexa said, "I think I might be okay with it if you want to have sex with Jada."

"What?"

"She's crazy sexy," Alexa declared. "And horny. My goodness, she is so horny. Now that we're close friends I believe I can deal with you getting pleasure in her arms. It helps that her attitude about it is so good."

"I think she's playing you."

"In a way, yes. She's doing what is needed to get what she wants. But isn't that what we all do in life? I don't feel played. Instead, I feel like I've been greedy."

"Really?" I asked in surprise.

"Don't tell me you no longer find her attractive. If anything, you are hotter for her now than you were before. I feel like I'm keeping you both from what you want."

"No," I insisted. "What I want is you, Alexa. And for you to be extremely happy. My desire for Jada never needs to be acted upon. Surely I have made that clear."

"Yes, you have, my dear. And I know very well that you mean it. That just makes it much easier for me to concede. I'm going to talk to Jada tomorrow and let you know for sure."

CHAPTER FOURTEEN:

I woke up after just five hours of sleeping in with Alexa in my arms. I almost panicked in my new surroundings before I remembered what we had done. A new house, a new bed. A wonderful sexual experience with my woman. A strong sense of insecurity struck me because we had not done much to make sure we would be safe through the night. I needed to check on Riley and make sure our home was secure.

I crept out of the wonderfully soft queen size bed without disturbing my girl enough to wake her. Fortunately, everything in the house was just fine. Riley was still awake, reading a book she had find on the bookshelf in the living room. *Arrive*, the first book of a three novel series called *New Earth*, she told me. It was reportedly an imagined future for earth that did not quite match what ended up actually happening, but a good read just the same.

I appreciated the new girl taking the first watch and was a little surprised that I trusted her so easily. I suggested that Riley get some sleep, and she accepted it as an order. I then took a quick inventory of the lumber and counted all the windows that needed boarding up. We had plenty of plywood to do the job, plus support boards and hardware.

Jada woke up shortly before I finished the task and a while before Alexa. Already accustomed to my productive mentality she immediately asked what she could do to help. She was a good woman. I had no doubt about that. I appreciated her immensely. It was a good thing that Alexa was getting so close to her. Instead of giving my sexy friend some immediate work to do I greeted her with a friendly hug.

"Oh," she said. "That's a nice way to wake up. Did you two not take care of business last night?"

"No, we did," I replied. "I just wanted you to know how much I appreciate you. And, by the way, Alexa is going to talk to you today."

"Oh yeah? Did I go too far last night?"

"Not at all, apparently. She is actually considering.... Well, you'll have to talk to her about it, when she's ready."

"Okay...." she replied, obviously curious. "I look forward to that. In the meantime, what do we need to do to get this place secure?"

"Let's get the windows boarded up with plywood. There are dozens of boxes of good screws, and a few drills. We could probably get them all done this morning if we work together. I also want to put some two by fours across the doors going outside. We'll attach some wood to the door frames to hold the lumber in place, so we can just lift the board out of the way when needed."

"Good plan. I like it. Where's Riley?"

"She's in bed, I hope. She stayed awake while I was sleeping."

"And Alexa?"

"She's still in bed."

"It's kind of late waking up for her," Jada said. "Wear her out, did you?"

"Maybe," I answered without looking in her direction. I wanted to focus on my work list but couldn't resist the reply.

"Stud," was all she said in response. Then together we carried our supplies to the windows that needed covered up. We put off drilling in the screws until all of us were awake. Instead, we took down the curtains and rods carefully hoping to put them back up afterwards. Fortification without completely destroying the comfortable appearance of our new home was the goal.

A couple hours later Alexa walked up to me wearing my only dress shirt. It was left unbuttoned exposing her flat belly and black bra and panties. Her hair was a bit of a mess. She obviously did not seek out a mirror before coming to me for her morning hug. But she was utterly beautiful to me just the same.

"Love you," she said softly, lingering against my chest.

"Love you, too, sweetheart," I replied, not caring who else heard. Surely by this point everyone knew that I was in love with this wonderful young woman.

Then Alexa went to Jada and hugged her, as well. I don't remember that being her morning custom, but I was glad to see them getting along. "Love you, Jada," she then said.

"Love you, too, girl," Jada replied without hesitation. It was the first time I had heard them say that, but I knew that close female friends would say it to each other often. I expected her to ask my girl how she enjoyed our sex the night before, but she surprisingly refrained. The two most important women in my life then went to the kitchen to figure out breakfast for the group. We hadn't brought a lot of food, but we were very fortunate that the pantry there was abundantly well stocked.

A little while later Riley joined us, and we had our first meal together in our new dwelling. A long maple table centered the dining area with an open view to the living room, kitchen and the backyard. Of course, the outdoor view was about to go bye-bye. Couldn't take a chance on someone breaking through the glass. Ten fine dining chairs surrounded the table, light maple wood with a padded white seat. It was quite an upgrade from our previous dining atmosphere.

By late afternoon the windows and doors were secured to my satisfaction and I began a new work list for the next day. I knew it would be important to plan our outhouse arrangement carefully if we intended to stay here for a while. Security and privacy were key, but also sanitation. Maybe one day we'll have the luxury of plumbing again. Until then, we will have to make doo as best we can. Ha-ha, I chuckled at my own word play.

After we put our tools and supplies away, the girls started cleaning up any mess we had made with our project. I was very pleased that we had no lazy members to our clan. Most of the time I didn't even need to ask anyone to perform a particular task, they sought out the work on their own. Despite her more fragile stature, Riley did not shy away from the physical work either.

I went in search of a way to enter the attic space. I noticed some small windows and vents from the outside the day before. There had to be some pull down hatch with possibly a ladder somewhere. It turns out that there were two, one between Jada and Riley's bedrooms, the other inside the laundry room. The second had a nice ladder that I could leave down permanently. The oven like temperatures above the main level in the poorly vented space hit me immediately. I glanced around to take a mental picture of the area before heading back down the ladder. Maybe the next day I would be more energetic and prepared to deal with that heat. There would be suitable peep holes in all directions from up there. I couldn't ignore the advantages of that just bird's nest view because of a little discomfort.

When I reentered the living room all three girls greeted me with smiles. They had finished their work and were ready for some recreation time. They didn't even have to say it. The pool cue in Jada's left hand, combined with the bottle of vodka in her right pretty much said it all.

"Oh, are we ready to shoot some pool?" I asked. I had to admit that I was looking forward to breaking in the game room. Ever since the comet struck the earth and started this series of attacks on our survival there hadn't been any real fun, except for our card games. And the sex, of course. I did enjoy my intimate time with Alexa very much. She was easily the most serious relationship in my life.

"I'm ready for you to teach me, master," Jada replied, seductive as always.

"How about you, Riley? Have you ever shot pool before?"

"No," Riley answered as if she were surprised that I thought she might have some billiards experience. "In fact, this might be my first time in a room with a pool table."

"I've played once before," Alexa added.

"Yeah, well I've only played a couple times myself," I lied. They weren't fooled, though. All three of them instantaneously expressed doubt in the truth of my statement.

I took a few minutes to cover with the girls some basic stuff about shooting pool, like always hit the cue ball first, where to find the balls that had dropped. Jada thought that expression hilarious. Then I patiently explained the rules for eight ball. I figured that would be the easiest game for them to learn and it could possibly even be somewhat competitive. Eventually, I shared with them something that most new players never get taught. That was how to aim so you could strike the target ball at the appropriate angle to propel it in the intended direction. The final instructions were going to be the most fun, though. How to hold and shoot the cue stick.

"Alexa, let me show you first."

"Why?"

"Because you are my girlfriend and the lesson does involve some close body contact."

"Oh," she replied with a smile. "In that case, definitely start with Jada. She is itching for some close body contact."

"Are you sure?" I asked, hesitant to obey. I did make myself clear about the physicality of the exercise, right?

Alexa nodded firmly so I welcomed Jada over to the table. She was indubitably ready for some schooling. I first demonstrated the position and technique then told her to try. Her hot body bent over and stroking the pool cue repeatedly against her breast had me distracted for a moment. Eventually, she asked, "Am I doing it right?"

"You must be," Alexa responded, laughing outright, "because Mason is drooling."

"Mason!" Jada feigned surprise.

"Sorry, yes, you look good. Maybe bend over a little more so you can see down the pool cue to aim."

"Show me," she winked. My girlfriend waved me toward the dark-skinned hottie, so I went. When I took my instructive place behind her she rubbed her firm ass against my now bulging privates. I had to back off to keep things from getting out of hand.

"I think you have it," I stuttered, turning away hoping no one got a good look at my pants. Unfortunately, I turned directly to face Riley. She just smiled, though. Always respective, never seductive. I could count on Riley. "Are we ready for a game?" I asked the group.

"Aren't we going to have drinks while we play?" Alexa asked.

"Sure, I can fix those," I said happily, appreciating how getting behind the bar could help hide my arousal.

"No, I'll get them." Riley floated to the liquor dispensary before me. "You go ahead and rack your balls so we can get the fun going."

"Oh my God!" Alexa said. "Did Riley just make a sexual joke?"

When the laughter died down, we began our first game of eight ball. I took Riley as my partner since we all figured that she might have the least amount of success at this point. That put Alexa tag teaming with Jada, which was something they might be doing with me soon if Alexa decided to share your lover. I sunk all our balls and the eight ball to only two of their balls going in. The second game was a little closer, but I still won. I mean, Riley and I won. She even pocketed a ball in that game. After that, Alexa and Jada kept coming up with silly rules to prevent me from dominating the game. Finally, I lost the seventh game to them. I had a very difficult time operating the pool cue one handed as they required with a good buzz on.

The drinks were flowing nicely as we had our fun, and everybody was at least a little tipsy. It was funny to see how touchy Riley got when she was drinking. Nothing sexual, mind you, but she had to touch your arm every time she was speaking to you. And she gave the other girls a few hugs with unusual timing as well.

Alexa was having way too much to drink, in my opinion. I knew that she would fall asleep immediately when we went to bed. I didn't need sex every day, but the way things were going there in the game room, my body was clearly anticipating something.

"Sweetie," I said to Alexa, pulling her aside once again. "Did you want some water? Or something more to eat?"

"No, Mason," she answered with a slur. "I know. I know. I won't be in good shape to have sex with you tonight. But, that's okay because I don't need the attention tonight."

"Oh," was all I could say.

"You, however, will be getting plenty of sex," she said. "I doubt that Jada will be too drunk to perform."

"I'm not comfortable with you making that decision while you are drinking, Lexie."

"I didn't. I made it when I was sober earlier today. And Jada already knows, so don't sweat it."

"Still...." I said.

"Mason, I love you very much. And I love Jada, just not in the same way, of course. But it would be devastating if Jada left us to go find herself a man. I think you should do it. We'll be okay. I'm sure of it."

It wasn't much later that Alexa orchestrated our opportunity. She declared that she was ready for bed and asked Riley if she would walk her there. Riley, of course, offered to take first watch again. However, her tiny body was struggling with the alcohol more than anyone else's. She could barely walk. Jada declared that she would take first watch instead. But I announced that no one needed to stay up at night anymore. We had secured the building well enough that we shouldn't have to worry about it. So, the two thinner women wandered off to bed after giving Jada and I both hugs and sloppy kisses. Well, Riley's kisses were not sloppy at all. She still had that way of barely touching your lips.

"So," Jada said, leaning against the pool table.

"So," I replied, leaning beside her. "I understand that you and Alexa had a talk."

"Yes, we did."

"She didn't mention it to me until just a few minutes ago. Were there any rules that I should know about?"

"Rules?" Jada asked. "You mean like no kissing? Or, that I couldn't orgasm? No, of course not. We are free to do as we please. I just need to respect that she is your first and most important woman. In fact, in case you are not aware of it, she considers herself your wife. And, for the record, so do I. I have a lot of respect for that woman of yours. The way I see it, being your second choice here is a much better option for me than anything I could hope for out there. It took a while for me to humble myself to the point that I could appreciate that. Now, here I am."

"I understand," I nodded. "So, how do we go about this?"

"Nervous?"

"Kind of."

"Well, don't be," she whispered as she moved in front of me. I was still ass up against the billiards table. She spread her legs to put her knees to the outside of mine, resting her rock-hard abdomen against my crotch as she caressed my chest and shoulders. When she looked into my eyes from that position, I could not deny her amazing beauty. Or her incredible sexiness. Or even how much I desired her. We kissed softly. And again. We literally spent several minutes mostly kissing. Oh, our hands wandered, of course. I had my fingers all over her back, arms, and then her ass. My God, what a perfect ass she had. Her hands wandered likewise, caressing my upper body, eventually grabbing me gently through my shorts.

I continued to kiss her passionately as she pulled my erection out to stroke. Her top came off then to reveal her award-winning breasts. Before I could reach for her shorts she had dropped to her knees. Her oral skills were well beyond anything I had ever experienced, or even knew were possible. I had to stop her before she went too far. Once completely naked I returned the favor, bringing her to a screaming orgasm. It didn't even take that long. We both wanted this so bad.

We left our clothes scattered on the game room floor as she led me by the hand to her bedroom. If the other girls were awake and about it would have been quite a sight to see. She pulled back the sheets and sat down on the edge of the bed, guiding me to her mouth once again.

"No," I said. "I'm too excited."

"Okay," she whispered. "I just want to do a very good job for you. How do you want me then?"

I guided her to a missionary position and tried to take it slow. My passion for this cocoa goddess was too much, though, and I kept raising her sexy legs up. I had to stop myself short time and time again. Then, I had her on all fours facing the headboard as I entered her from behind. The view again was so incredible that I didn't last but a minute. When I reached the point of no return, she joined me, screaming out once again.

After that superlative performance we laid there for a while silently, her head on my chest. I caressed her silky skin so softly. I never believed that the color of a person's skin or their race determined anything about them. But Jada's skin felt so smooth it was just felt like candy to my touch, matching its chocolate appearance.

"Are we okay?" Jada finally asked.

"Sure," I replied hesitantly, not really expecting the question in the first place.

"I hope so," she said. "I love you both and don't want to hurt either of you. Please take care of Alexa so she doesn't regret her decision."

"I will. I promise."

"Good," she said. "So, when can we do this again?"

"I don't know. Let's see how Alexa feels tomorrow and the next day. Hopefully, we can get together soon.

"I would like that," she said as she kissed my chest again.

"I'll try to last much longer next time."

"Why?" Jada asked. I figured she was trying to protect my ego. "Hey, I had a fantastic time. I wouldn't change a thing."

"Me, too. Me, too."

Shortly thereafter I dismissed myself and went back to my room where Alexa was sound asleep. I tried not to wake her but couldn't resist putting my arm around her slender waist causing her to stir.

"Sorry to wake you sweetie. Love you."

"Love you, too, Mason. So, how did it go?"

"Did you want to know the details?"

"No, not really. I just want to know if you both got what you needed out of it. And," she hesitated, "if you still want me."

"Oh goodness, Alexa. I want you more than ever. You are the prefect woman, really."

"Yeah?" I could tell she was working up her nerve to say something. Then, "Would I make a good wife?"

"The best," I answered. I could be a little dim witted sometimes, but at that moment I knew what she wanted. What she needed. What we both needed, really, to make this new world work properly for us.

I tilted her headed so she could look me in the eyes. Then said, "Alexa, you are the love of my life, and I always want you with me. Would you do me the great honor of being my wife?"

She cried. Then she nodded. Then she cried some more. Finally, she said through the tears, "Yes, Mason. I would love to be your wife."

I fell asleep thinking, "what a perfect day."

CHAPTER FIFTEEN:

I began the next morning in the arms of the most wonderful woman on the planet, once again. She held me so tight that I couldn't bring myself to get out of bed, despite my work list calling me. Eventually, Alexa declared that it was time for coffee. We started our new morning routine together. I checked to make sure the building was secure as she started up our hot coffee process and figured out breakfast.

Once Jada and Riley joined us, I made my way upstairs before it got too hot up there. I kept my greeting with my new athletic lover brief intentionally so as not to offend my wife. Jada seemed to understand quickly, but still managed to plant a brief smooch on my lips before I broke the embrace. I had no idea if the kiss went unnoticed as I was heading for the ladder already.

There were suitable peek holes in all directions in the attic. Some adjustments would need to be made to enable me to use the binoculars easily through two of the vents, but I was happy with the situation overall. I couldn't spot any human forms in our new yard, but there were a few deer, and some rabbits. So far, we were off to a very good start in our new home. We had chosen the place without doing extensive recon on the area. For all we knew we put ourselves in a hotbed of rotter or clan activity. But there was no evidence to suggest that yet.

Breakfast was ready when I returned downstairs. I could smell the coffee easily as well as something made with cinnamon. Riley was in the process of setting the dining room table with plates and silverware. This house was not only better than our place at the old beer store, it was much nicer than the home I grew up in. I began to feel like a king, especially with the affection of Alexa and Jada, as well as the respect and admiration of Riley.

I declared to my devoted women that I had chosen Alexa as my wife and was prepared to have a ceremony. However, Alexa made it clear that a formal arrangement would not be necessary. She did insist that I get her a decent ring, though. I could find it in a house, or steal it from a store, she didn't care, but it had to fit. And it had to be "wow". I put the task at the top of my list.

As the day continued, I couldn't help but notice that Alexa was acting a little differently around Jada. She was keeping her emotional distance, so to speak. I guessed that it was to be expected, but I feared how much damage to our group dynamic may have been done by my sexual escapade the night before. I made a concerted effort to show more affection to the one and less to the other. Jada gave me a stare and a weak smile that I assumed meant that she understood what was going on but was not at all happy about it. Shortly after that I was able to overhear the two women talking in the other room when Jada finally had the opportunity to approach Alexa in private.

"Alexa? Are we okay?"

"Sure," Alexa replied, unconvincingly.

"I can tell that you are not happy with me," Jada said. "I'm sorry if I have offended you. I tried my best to only do what you allowed."

"I know," Alexa said. "It's my own fault. I'm the one that made the decision to allow you to have sex with my man. I can't help feeling now like it may have been a mistake. Maybe I'll get over it eventually."

"What can I do?" Jada asked.

"Nothing."

"Alexa, please. Talk to me. I want to make this work for all of us. If you're not happy, I'm not happy. And I know Mason will not be happy. What can I do?"

"I said, nothing! There is nothing anyone can do now. The deed is done," Alexa choked out as she started to cry. I refrained from rushing into the room to comfort her. Peeking around the corner, though, I could see that Jada was already giving her a hug, and Alexa received it without issue. It was a while before they spoke again, but I waited patiently.

"So, did the two of you have a good time last night?" Alexa asked without looking directly at her friend.

"I'm not going to lie, Alexa. I had a great time. Thank you so much for sharing. I know that is not an easy thing to do. You are a strong and brave woman, despite how you are feeling right now."

"Did he have any hesitation at least?" Alexa asked.

"Girl," Jada replied. "Make no mistake about it. Mason loves you more than anything else in this world. And that will never change. You can be confident of that."

"Do you love him, too?"

Jada hesitated, then took a deep breath. "Yes, I think I might. But that doesn't mean that I will try to take him from you."

"How long can you stay happy being his second woman?" Alexa asked. "I don't think I could do it."

"We're in a new world and I have to make adjustments. We all do. Even Mason. Do you think he would even consider having a second lover if things were still the same as before? No way. He is devoted to you."

"If I change my mind and want to keep him to myself, will that cause you to leave us?"

"Maybe. I don't know. I don't want to go."

"I don't want you to go, either," Alexa replied, pulling Jada close again for another embrace.

"Then let's make this work, dear," Jada said. "Let's make it work the best we can for all of us. I want to help and support you in every way I can. Just, please, don't shut me out."

When the two of them came back into the living area I pretended like I had no idea what they were talking about. Unfortunately, I was a terrible liar. And Alexa would know anyway. Hell, she probably knew I was eavesdropping just by reading my emotions while they were talking. She had gotten very good at not letting it affect her.

"I need to go on a quick supply run," I announced. "I think I'll just take Riley with me this time."

"No, I should go, too," Alexa insisted. "You need me to sense danger."

"Not this time, I think. Between Riley's speed burst and my deflection ability, I think we'll be alright. You two should stay here and chill out."

"You don't think I'm able to help you in my current emotional state," Alexa stated. "I get it. I disagree, but I appreciate where you are coming from. But why not take Jada?"

"I want her here so you two can protect each other while I'm gone. We should avoid having any of us on their own from now on."

"And," Alexa stated. "You don't want me here by myself wondering what you and Jada are doing together elsewhere. Okay."

"Mason is a smart leader," Riley announced.

Jada barred the door securely after we exited. We came up with a knock system that would let each other know who it was at the door. That was just in case we had to be too quiet to be heard through the boarded windows verbally. Some of them walkie talkies would probably come in handy now that our clan was growing. I would have to keep an eye out for some. I carried Jada's hatchet with me while Riley brought along the small baseball bat. I also took Earl's rifle this time. I was not comfortable using a gun, or shooting to kill, but maybe it would help ward off would be attackers.

"What kind of supplies do we need, Mason?" Riley asked as we walked tentatively around the pool house.

"None, really, but we'll grab anything useful while we're out."

"Then what is our primary objective, if you don't mind me asking."

"I need to get Alexa an engagement ring. I imagine we can worry about wedding bands later. I think that a big ring on her finger might go a long way in stabilizing our household," I said. "I assume that you already know about Jada and I spending some time together last night."

"Yes, I have been told that the two of you had sex," she replied as if it was of no serious consequence. "But I thought it had already been agreed upon. It came as no surprise when Jada told me this morning."

"Jada told you, did she? What all did she say?"

"Not much, that I can repeat comfortably. She did say that you were a great unselfish lover."

"Well, that was nice of her. How do you read this situation between Jada and Alexa? I mean our love triangle. I'd really like to know more than what I can see for myself, if you don't mind talking about it."

Riley paused. For a moment I thought she might refuse to reveal anything useful. I couldn't blame her. I always tried to stay out of other people's messes. It seemed like you were more likely to make things worse anyway. But now, the way things were. I might not even be alive if Alexa had stayed out of my mess back when I faced Earl and the two girls. Jada probably wouldn't be alive if we didn't get involved when she was surrounded by the stinkies at the church.

"I will tell you anything that you want to know, of course."

"Riley," I said as I stopped so we could talk face to face. "I appreciate how respectful you are to me. I really do. But sometimes, it feels a little subservient. And that I don't particularly like. We will probably never get to be as close as I am with Alexa or Jada, but I would like for you to start treating me more like a friend and less like your master. Can you do that for me?"

"Of course," she replied in her normal tone. "I did not mean to offend..."

"No, no! This is what I'm talking about. Wait, let's take a seat over there in the shade where we won't be easily spotted. I want to talk this out now." I guided the elegant waif to a group of bushes beneath two large trees. We wouldn't be visible to passersby from most angles there. I sat cross-legged on the grass and Riley did the same facing me, our knees nearly touching. I took both of her thin, delicate hands in mine as I spoke.

"Do you understand what I am asking of you?"

"Yes," Riley replied. "I do understand. And I will do my best. But please, I am who I am. Some things are hard for me to change. I will always treat you like my leader. However, I believe that I can make some changes that would satisfy you. I want to communicate anything I know to you because I want our clan to be its strongest, and happiest. I believe that you would make good use of any knowledge that I provide. So, what would you like to know?"

"How does Alexa feel about me?"

"From what I can tell, she still loves you very much. She is very excited to be officially named your wife."

"How does she feel about Jada?"

"I don't think that she resents Jada really. Her presence though is a reminder of what has happened between you two. It may take her some time for that to fade. Their friendship is very strong, I believe."

"How does Jada feel about this new arrangement?"

"She is delighted, of course. She gets to have sex with you. She will continue to do her best to behave, though it is not easy for her. She wants to respect your relationship with Alexa, but in time she might not be satisfied with being the second woman. She has always been a strong independent person. This new world of ours has forced her to make some changes, but none of us can change overnight. I advise that you tread softly in this area. I doubt that you will ever lose either woman, but it might require all your social skills to keep things consistently peaceful."

"Wow," I said. "Once again you have said more than I have expected. And it's awesome. I appreciate it. What else can you tell me?"

"I think that you are right about getting an engagement ring for Alexa. It should help considerably. I also recommend that you sleep in Alexa's bed every night regardless of who your sexual partner was. Maybe, eventually, Alexa will feel strong enough in your relationship that you could spend the entire night in Jada's bed, or in mine for that matter."

"Yours?"

"I am a woman, too, Mason. I might not make sexual advances like Jada, but in time I'm sure I will welcome you into my bed. It is inevitable. You are a good and handsome man. Both of your women speak well of you, particularly in your love making ability. I am becoming a devoted follower of yours. It is bound to happen."

"Okay," I replied, a little shy once again. "Thanks for sharing that. Right now, I have my hands full with Alexa and Jada, but we should revisit this sometime in the future. Okay?"

"Yes, of course. I know neither of us are ready for that step. It is much too early in our relationship. We are only speaking of it because I let it slip out to help you understand that Alexa is a stronger woman than she thinks she is. In time, she will grow into her new role as your first woman instead of your only woman."

"Thanks, for all that you have said, Riley. This helps a lot. Is there anything that I can do for you? I mean to make you feel more comfortable with our clan?"

"I have been made to feel welcome by all of you."

"Can you think of anything that you would like? Please, tell me of any tiny change that could make you happier."

"Okay. Since you really want to know. There are a few things that I would like."

"Great, what can I do?" I believed I was getting good at how to deal with Riley. She would open up to me if I was patient but persistent. Her natural supportive tendency was a huge asset to my clan.

"First," she began. "I would prefer to have an assignment, like a permanent responsibility. It would be my primary contribution to the clan. Assisting Alexa with the cooking, and Jada with security is good, but I'd like to feel like I am a fixed part of the group, that everyone is counting on me."

"Sure. I can see that. We'll talk about what works best and make that happen. Right now, I've been keeping track of our supply inventory. Is that something that you would like to take over?"

"Yes, that would be perfect. Thank you. Once we get back, I'd like for you to show me where everything is, and I'll keep track from now on. You will all be able to count on me."

"I know we will," I replied. "What else can I do?"

"I would like for you to get more comfortable at giving me orders. I know that is not how you like to lead, and I respect that. However, I like to be productive, especially early in the day. I have a fear of overstepping my rightful place, so I don't take on tasks often unless you assign them to me. I'm sure that eventually I will get more comfortable at it. Until then, please tell me anything that you would like for me to do."

"I will try," I answered. "Remind me, please. In fact, you can ask me for something to do anytime you want. Is there anything else I can do for you?"

Riley bowed her head slightly, hesitating. I waited patiently. "Yes, there is one more thing. It's not very important, but I guess now is my opportunity to speak up. I am a bit envious of Alexa and Jada."

"Oh? How so?"

"You are a very friendly man, and you show that by touching people when you talk to them. And hugging often. I know that we are not as close. And I know that my manner can sometimes be off putting. I have noticed that you refrain from being as friendly with me, almost treating me like I am too fragile."

"I'm sorry."

"Don't be. It's not your fault. You are doing what you think is right based on the information in front of you. I'm just not very good at expressing myself in that way. Seeing you with the other two, though, makes me want to change. I'm afraid that I can't do it on my own. So, I only ask that you not hold back from making physical contact when appropriate. I believe you fear that I will not appreciate it, but I will."

"Okay, that's cool," I said. "I will do my best. How about a hug right now before we get back on our mission?"

"I would like that."

After standing I reached for Riley as I stepped forward. She was right. Her hesitation was off putting. I surely got the vibe that she didn't want to be touched. I ignored it and pulled her close. She didn't resist, so I held her to my chest for a few seconds. I could feel her thin arms tightening around my waist. As I released. I gave her a quick peck on the cheek. I had the feeling that her comfort level was so much lower because the other girls were not around. Her timid smile as I stepped back told me all I needed to know.

"Was that good?"

"Perfect," she whispered shyly.

From that point on Riley walked a little closer to me and didn't trail behind as she was accustomed. We continued to talk as we went, mostly about our lives before and after the catastrophe. The walk between the houses allowed for more conversation than the two of us alone had time for previously. It quickly became obvious to me that we were going to be great friends.

We focused on finding a nice ring first as we searched every house, then gather supplies that we could carry in our backpacks. It wasn't until approaching the fourth home that we had any trouble. There was a grunt type of barking happening in the front yard. We moved stealthily through the bushes on the side of the house to get a better view. We could smell the problem before we could see it. Two skunks were apparently arguing, each supported by several skanks at their back. I could make out some of the words once we were closer.

"Grunt grunt fucking grunt shit grunt," one said.

"You no good piece of grunt grunt, that my bitch grunt, give my grunt bitch back or I grunt grunt fuck you grunt," the other replied. Some of the guttural noises may have actually been grunts instead of unrecognizable words.

I gathered that they were fighting over followers. The so-called bitch in question then shook her fist at the skunk wanting her back. She then pointed at her ass and said something that may have been "spank too hard." I saw a couple of the skanks that had not yet jumped ship nod their heads. I deduced that the skunk that had trouble holding on to his women liked to spank them during sex. Since their bodies didn't heal well, it was an ongoing ache after the experience. Now the question was if the spanker could fight, because the other skunk wasn't backing down.

The protective skunk held a table leg in one hand with two bolts sticking out of the top end. In his other hand was a metal trash can lid that was obviously going to be his shield. The spanker held a golf club in his right hand, a big-headed driver, and a French-chef's knife in his left.

"Have you seen anything like this before?" I whispered my question to Riley.

"Yes, I have. It can get very nasty. I prefer not to watch. In the city, some of the clan lords will have these zombie-like people battle for their lives coliseum style for their entertainment."

"That's awful," I replied, a little louder than I should have. One of the closest skanks looked our way for a couple seconds. Fortunately, the continued grunting of the skunks drew her attention back to the impending battle. We took the opportunity to sneak back the way we came and then headed across the street to continue our search.

In the fifth house we searched since crossing the street we found lots of jewelry in a dresser drawer, concealed in felt bags. There were several rings, including a solitaire engagement ring and a wedding band. They were just barely too big for Riley's slender fingers, so I estimated that they would fit Alexa perfectly. I pocketed the two special items that hopefully would be precious to my primary woman. Then I tossed the rest in my backpack after allowing Riley to select a nice necklace for herself.

The trip back to our new luxury home was trickier than usual. Skanks were crawling out of the woodwork evidently, all headed toward the area where the two skunks were facing off. This was going to be one big nasty, rotten flash battle. The neighborhood was sure to stink for a while afterwards. I was glad that it wasn't close to our new place. I wanted to make haste to get clear of the ordeal but didn't want to attract any of their attention.

Just as we cleared a hill that enabled me to spot our house, solar panels shining in the sunlight, I heard barking off to my left. We had been noticed after all. At least a dozen of the zombie like women were headed our way, shuffling as best they could. The two skanks in the lead appeared as if they could possibly match our speed. We took off running for our house. We had to make it time for the girls to let us in.

When I began to slow down for Riley to catch up, she yelled, "keep going! I'll catch up soon. Go!"

I trusted her statement to be true despite my doubts and sped up. One of us would have to reach the door as fast as possible anyway. Hopefully, Riley would not stumble and fall. That would surely enable the skanks to catch her, at least those first two. We could fight them off easily, I'm sure, but it would allow time for the others to catch up. Even if we could beat them all, they would sustain injuries from which they could not heal, possibly even die. I wanted to avoid causing anymore death, if it was in my power. There was also the chance of us getting hurt.

I was almost fifty feet from the front door when a black-haired blur flew by me on the right. Riley had used her speed burst to not only catch up, as she had promised. She surpassed me and made it to the entrance before me. I joined her in yelling for help as we pounded our special knock loud enough to get the girls attention. Hopefully they could sense our urgency enough to let us in as quick as they could. I turned to see the two lead skanks almost upon as I heard the door bar being slid out of place. Just then Riley passed out from over exertion of her skill and began to crumple to the floor. I caught her by her armpits and raised her up to hang over my shoulder lack a large sack of seeds.

Both stinky women raised the clubs in their hands as they closed the gap between us. Instinctively, I used my free hand to grab the large rubber door mat from below me and toss it in their direction. I followed it up with a wave of the same hand to deflect it at them at a much higher speed. They were plainly caught by surprise when the ten-pound rubber mat took them off their feet. I couldn't tell how badly they were hurt by my attack at first. They were not able to regain an upright position until after we were all inside and Jada had barred the door.

"Oh my God!" Alexa said. "Is Riley okay?"

"I think so," I replied, still trying to catch my breath. "She passed out from using her speed burst. Let me lay her on the couch."

"I told you I should have come with you!" Jada shouted.

A barrage of pounding on the front door drew our attention back to the situation at hand. Riley was awake then, but groggy. There was no sense in hovering over her. She would recover on her own in a few minutes. The sound of the glass windows on the front of the house shattering was muted by the plywood we had secured behind it, but it was still alarming.

"Can they get in?" Alexa asked panicky.

"Not easily," I replied.

"What do we do?" Jada asked, looking to me for orders. Her anger at being left at home had passed.

"We wait to see if they leave," I replied calmly.

"And if they don't?" Alexa asked.

"Then we'll have to chase them off," Jada answered for me. I nodded my agreement. "Just let me know when and what you want me to do."

CHAPTER SIXTEEN:

We left ourselves a few small peek holes when we boarded up the windows. Still our view was terribly limited. As best as I could tell, there were about fifteen skanks in our recently acquired yard, and no skunks. I couldn't make out a clear leader among the women, but some must have taken the initiative to circle our new home. A heavy blonde with nasty cuts on her puffy face was trying to figure out how to get into the back door. That wasn't going to happen. We had it barred up good. A slender brunette that might have been attractive if it weren't for her grayish skin and the nasty rash on her legs, was using a rock to bust every window. She was making her way clockwise around the building. The glass would shatter but the plywood held strong. Two others were trying to raise the garage door to no avail.

"Do they have to break every window?" Jada asked.

"They aren't going away," Alexa said, trying her best to stay calm. "I think that they are looking for food. The pain I'm picking up from them seems to be more than from their injuries. It's hard to tell, but they are clearly not happy."

"Yeah, they don't look happy," I replied. "I think we are going to have to chase them off. I was hoping to address their leader, but they don't appear to have one."

"What do you want me to do, Mason?" Jada asked, ready for battle.

"Get the weapons ready here by the front door. Riley, grab some crackers from the kitchen. Maybe if we give them some food they'll go away."

Riley returned quickly with three boxes of saltine crackers. "Here's some food for them, but Mason, I don't think this will make them go away. They'll probably just want more."

"So, you think we'll be wasting food by giving it to them?" I asked my newest clan member.

"I do, but I understand your desire to try a diplomatic approach first. However, I don't think they'll leave without being forced off."

"How do we do that without killing them?" Alexa asked Riley.

"I don't know," she replied somberly. "I have never seen it done without at least some casualties."

Great, I thought. Just great. I didn't want to kill anyone. I knew that these females were people despite their rotting flesh, hygiene issues and poor communication skills. I also knew that they didn't have a real chance of defeating us. Most of them had some sort of weapon in their hand, even if it were just a stick or a rock. How many would we have to fatally wound to get them to leave? Would killing more discourage them from ever coming back? How many rotting corpses did we really want in the yard of our new luxury home? Damn it! I didn't want to do this.

"Ok," I told my women, "grab your weapons of choice. Let's look strong. Maybe that will be enough to scare them off. If not, we'll injure a few to get our point across. Try not to get into psycho warrior battle mode, Jada. I don't want to kill any more than necessary."

"Got it," Jada replied without taking any offense.

"Riley. I know you are still a little weak. Stay behind us at first. How long before your speed burst is ready?"

"Maybe in a few more minutes, if you can stall them. But, using it that quick again will probably knock me out."

"Okay, don't use it unless I say."

"We're coming out!" I yelled to the zombie like bitches outside. "Get away from the door!"

Alexa reported that they were eventually following my repeated instructions to vacate the front porch as she watched through the nearest peep hole. Jada and I exited first, then Riley and Alexa. My size, gender and spear seemed to intimidate them a little. Jada's confident stance combined with her spear and axe helped as well. The smaller two girls each just carried a baseball bat and lacked any capacity for intimidation.

"Alexa, are they scared of us yet?"

"Some of them are, but not all. I think the red-haired woman in the middle might be the closest thing they have to a leader."

"Red!" I shouted at the pale redhead that Alexa pointed out. She clearly knew that I was talking to her. "You and your horde need to leave. I can give you some crackers to help with your hunger, but no more. Do you understand?"

"We take all we grunt grunt," she replied, as best as I could tell. With that she took two steps forward. Half of the other skanks did the same, but some were clearly hesitant.

"I don't want to have to kill you," I said as I pointed my spear directly at Red. She was still a good eight feet away.

Red then pulled a bowie knife out of her thick leather belt and growled through missing teeth, "Kill you!"

Two of the rancid women then stepped forward as if given a command, one on each side of us. The petite skank on the left had a shiny iron golf club. Why were these things so popular as weapons? She also had short black hair and a shitload of tattoos. Her left arm was kept discernably close to her torso and had a nasty cut from her wrist to her elbow. Other than that, she looked reasonably healthy. The one on the right was a much heavier girl with long brown hair and a wicked scowl. She banged together the two rocks that she held in her hands like a clapping toy monkey. She limped a little, but not enough to keep her from rushing us.

Jada was to my right, so she prepared to deal with the bigger girl. The inked-up chick reached me first though.

I dodged the swing of her golf club and responded by striking her head with the butt end of my spear. The blow was hard enough to more than knock her off her feet. She practically did a cartwheel before landing on the ground. She was dazed, but not unconscious.

I turned to see what was happening with Jada as I heard the disgusting guttural noise of her victim. Jada had plummeted the spearhead deep into her belly. The big girl dropped her rocks and clutched the shaft of the spear with both hands as blood came from her mouth. Some of the remaining skanks were in utter shock, but not Red. She ran right at me with two more of her friends right on her tail. I tried the same maneuver as I used on the previous girl, hesitant to deliver a fatal blow. She deflected my spear with her baseball bat and continued until she struck my chest with her shoulder. Perhaps she thought that she could tackle me. I barely took a backwards step before bringing my weapon down across her back, crosschecking style. She screamed as she dropped to the ground on her hands and knees before me.

Alexa swung her bat and completely missed her weaponless attacker. Instead, that girl dove at my sweetheart with claws extended forward. She barely made contact before I harpooned her in the back, causing her to arch up and withdraw from her attack.

Riley stood motionless with her wooden bat raised straight up in front of her, more like a shield than a weapon. Her eyes grew large as the skank launched herself with a battle cry right at her, swinging the tree branch in her hand. Than Jada's hatchet nearly took the stinker's head clean off. She managed to kill Riley's attacker while still holding the spear that was stuck in the heavy girl's bleeding gut. Ignoring my instructions to minimize the killing, Jada had clearly snapped into warrior mode. Considering the surprising strength of our enemy, it was a good thing.

When Red clutched at my legs and made to start biting my ankle, I brought the pointy end of my weapon down with great force. It went directly through her heart, pinning her and my spear to the ground. Jada then used her foot to pry her primary weapon out of the big stinker's belly causing the woman to tumble backwards clutching her wound. Once again, she had two weapons ready.

The tattooed girl had gotten back to her feet but obviously had no interest in rejoining the battle. With one hand to the side of her head she backed away slowly. Half of the remaining skanks did the same, while the rest of them scurried off as quick as their afflicted bodies could take them. We had won the battle, as I expected. But we had four dead skanks at our feet. The stench was already almost unbearable. It would only get worse.

As if on cue, Alexa started to puke. Riley was struggling to fight back the urge herself.

"Back inside, girls," Jada ordered them before I had the chance. "Mason and I will get this cleaned up."

"No," Riley responded, covering her mouth with her hand. "I will help."

"Alexa? Are you hurt?" I saw blood on her arm but didn't know for sure if it was hers. The beautiful blond wiped her mouth with one arm as she looked where I was pointing on the other.

"Oh God!" she muttered just before she passed out. Jada and I caught her together before she could hit the ground. We carried her inside and placed her gently on the sectional sofa as Riley barred the door. Jada then ran to get a couple bottles of water and a wash cloth. Using one of the bottles to wet the cloth she started wiping Alexa's face, then addressed the wound on her arm. I was still holding my wife's hand when she woke up to see Jada cleaning her injury.

"How bad is it?" Alexa asked.

"Not as bad as your leg was cut," I answered. "You healed remarkably fast from that. I'm sure you'll be fine."

"Yeah, but this cut came from a skank," Jada said. "Do you think that Alexa got contaminated with anything?"

"Oh no!" Alexa cried.

"Relax," I said. "Remember, they are not zombies or vampires. There is no reason to think they can contaminate a victim with a scratch or a bite. Thanks Jada. That's all we need right now."

"Sorry," she replied earnestly as she bandaged Alexa's arm. Alexa didn't seem completely convinced yet, but my logic was solid. She would see soon enough when nothing drastic happened.

With that done I decided to switch our focus to the task outside. "Let's get those bodies far from the house before they stink any worse, if that's possible, or draw wild animals to us. Jada, do we have anything we can wear for masks to keep us from getting nauseous?"

"I can get those," Riley offered, jogging gracefully into another room. She would soon be taking over the responsibility for our supplies. It was good to see her jumping at the opportunity.

"I want to help clean up," Alexa stated as she stood up. She didn't appear shaky. As long as she didn't start throwing up again, she could feasibly be of valuable assistance. The injured arm was not enough for me to exclude her.

"Are you sure?" I asked. Alexa nodded.

"That's my strong girl," Jada said as she gathered our weapons by the door. Alexa gave her friend's back a stare like she felt the condescending tone. Riley returned with paper masks designed for keeping out paint fumes, and some handkerchiefs. A minute later we were all geared up like doctors or bandits to go back outside.

"We all need to carry our weapons and be on guard. The skanks might not have wandered far."

As soon as we stepped outside the odor hit us like a slap in the face. Even the masks couldn't make it bearable for long. We would have to do this thing quickly, but not carelessly. I grabbed a heavy tarp from the garage to minimize how much we would have to handle the corpses, and two sets of garden gloves. Jada and I worked together to lift two bodies onto the tarp. The worst part was picking up any chunks of decaying flesh that had fallen off the body. It was even more than disgusting than it sounds.

Jada and I then walked backwards pulling the tarp as the other two girls lifted the trailing end to minimize drag. Any weapons that we couldn't carry we tossed onto the tarp with the bodies. Our goal was to take this mess as far as the tall grass on the perimeter of the property. I guessed it to be about three hundred feet. Our method eased the process, but the smell just made everything more difficult.

I had us stop for a break after the first hundred feet. I scouted the area for any skanks that might think that was a good time to re-attack. Nothing so far. I wished I had thought to bring the binoculars. Riley thought that she saw movement over by the neighbor's large house, but whatever it was must have moved on before I could see it. Hopefully it was an animal that had not been infected. I had enough of killing for a while.

Eventually we made it to the tall grass and dumped the putrid bodies. Still two more nasty corpses to go. I wanted to quickly add them to the pile before scavenger beasts started showing up. Riley caught some movement again as we headed back to our house. This time I was able to catch a glimpse as well. Neither of us were able to make out any details, though. It appeared to be a human form at quick glance. Best hurry up, just in case.

Though we were tiring quickly I urged the girls to put everything they had into the task at hand. I promised them a fun relaxing time back inside the house after this nauseating chore was complete. As we dumped the two remaining bodies Alexa perked up, beautiful blue flashing on her face the same brilliant color as her big eyes. However, I knew the meaning of the scene was undesirable. She was sensing someone nearby.

"What's up?" I asked her.

"People," she said, turning to look where we had seen the movement earlier. We all followed her lead and looked at the hill upon which the next house was built. Four people then stood there, unafraid, weapons in hand.

"Skanks?" Jada asked, hopeful. Regular or gifted people would be much more of a challenge.

"No," Alexa replied. "It's another clan, I think. They are not afraid of us. Some are eager to fight."

"At least it's just four of them." Jada said.

"No, there are more!" Alexa declared. "They are trying to surround us!"

"Grab the weapons. Run!" I yelled, dropping the tarp. All four of us headed for our house as quickly as we could. I started to run ahead to give me time to undo the rigging we had set up in the door to slow down any intruders while we were disposing of the bodies. I was still at least fifty feet from the building when I saw the others. Five more attackers came around the left corner of our house, then four more around the right. The people we had spotted next door had started jogging in our direction when we bolted and were nearly upon us as well.

"Thirteen," Jada counted for us once everyone was caught up and standing by my side. Perhaps she was calculating our odds or forming her own defense strategy. Stating the number of attackers, however, simply clarified for me that we were completely overwhelmed. They were not skanks, nor were they simple-minded beasts. This was an experienced clan with members skilled in combat.

"Alexa?" I queried. "Do they just want to talk?"

"No," she replied, trembling from fear and the emotions she was picking up. "They intend to kill you Mason."

CHAPTER SEVENTEEN:

"I imagine that they want to kill us all," Jada said.

"No," Riley replied. "That is not the way of things these days. They would ultimately prefer to eliminate Mason and adopt the three of us women into their clan. They won't hesitate to kill some of us if they must. However, they want to leave with something of value. Some of us must be spared to make the risk of battle worthwhile."

"She's right," Alexa added. "Us girls are the spoils of war."

Thirteen enemies versus us four. The numbers were not good at all. Chances were, they had much more combat experience as well. It was unknown what special powers they might have, unless Alexa could pick up on something. Perhaps we could stall enough to get some clues from their actions. The opposing clan was approaching cautiously. That might be to our advantage.

I did the quick math in my head. The odds of me surviving this conflict was slim to none. I was certain that Alexa and Jada would unselfishly give their lives fighting for me. Maybe Riley, too. It might be better to let them have the girls to save their lives. These aggressors might let me walk away. Or, I could run and use my dodging skills to get away alive. Only thing, I seriously doubted the girls would go for it.

"I think the three of you should consider surrendering. There is no need for you to die."

"Shut up!" Alexa blurted out. "Don't even think that! I wouldn't want to live without you."

"She's right," Jada added. "There is no chance that I'll surrender either. I'll fight to the death to protect you. Riley?"

"I'm in as well," Riley answered confidently.

Ok, that was not an option then. It made me feel good that these wonderful, beautiful women would give their lives for me, but awful that it would likely happen. I would have to do my absolute best to keep them all alive longer than me. They could reconsider their options after I'm dead. But how would I manage that against all these attackers? Could I bring myself to make a suicide run to protect them? I couldn't stand for that to be the last thing this world remembers me for.

Though there were three groups of enemies, the two groups on the right were almost close enough to be one large group of eight. That made the five people on the left the smaller group. But it wasn't that easy. Weapons, special skills, and even physical size had to be counted in to the strategy. We needed to determine the strongest adversaries and the leader. Alexa should be about to help with that.

"Give up your women and we'll let you go," the pistol toting man to the right of the house yelled out. He was a small guy with a long black beard coming to a gray point in the center of his chest. Since he spoke first, I assumed he was the leader.

"Is he in charge?" I whispered to Alexa.

"I believe so. But I don't think he intends to let you live if you agree. Don't do it Mason."

"Okay. As their leader, let's assume that he has a special ability in addition to the gun," I told my women. "The voluptuous woman in the sexy dress beside him has no weapon, so she definitely has an ability to watch out for."

"She's one of the most confident," Alexa added.

"And one of the women on the left is also empty handed."

"Well?" the bearded guy yelled again.

"How do I know that you'll let me live?" I asked the little shirtless guy in dirty khaki shorts. I needed to stall while we planned. He no doubt wouldn't wait much longer before attacking. He had the numbers and his clan was clearly prepared for battle.

"You don't" he replied with a smile that was then shared by many of his clan. "But what choice do you have?"

The four people that we spotted first on the hill were then on our far right. One was a large man in bib overalls carrying a hunting rifle. I believed the odds were best in favor of us focusing on the five to the left. We would then be going away from the gunfire of the two males.

"Alright," I told my supportive and beautiful clan. "We're going to charge the five on the left. Riley? Can you do mini bursts of speed, so you don't use up all your energy at once?"

"I can try," she answered.

"Good. You go for the small girl that doesn't have any weapons. Your possible immunity could make a big difference if she's gifted. Jada, you go for the big woman while I go for the tough looking guy. They both have swords, so I'll try to deflect their swings as we attack."

"Sounds good," Jada answered.

"What about me?" Alexa asked, obviously nervous.

"Our attack will leave one woman on each side. They both have baseball bats. They'll likely attack one of us while we're distracted. Pick one and whack the shit our of them with your bat."

Just then a gunshot got our attention. The clan leader had fired a shot into the air. "You have five seconds to decide!"

"Okay!" I yelled back. Then to my girls, "All three of you together, slowly reach down and grab those decorative pebbles at our feet while we pretend to lower our weapons. When I say so, toss them to the right and take off running for your target on the left." Then again, to our foe, "I give up! Let me put down my spear!"

I slowly dropped down in unison with the girls. I hoped it looked like we were going to surrender. Once they all three had a handful of pebbles I gave the command, "Now!"

We apparently succeeded in surprising them. None of them had their weapon ready as the girls threw the small beige rocks to our right. With a wave of my arm I deflected them at high speed toward the eight enemies in that general direction. As we sprinted for the clan members by the left corner of our house, I heard two gunshots. I did my best to push them upwards as they approached, though I couldn't be sure where they were headed. Quickly after that were a few screams. It was in the distance, so I deduced that some of them fuckers were struck by our barrage of pebbles.

The first four of our targets braced for battle, startled by our rush. The fifth was a young lady that was standing a little behind the other four all along, obviously less enthusiastic about fighting. She dropped her baseball as soon as we started her way and took off running in the other direction. Cool, that left us at just four on four.

I aimed for both the man with the sword and the weaponless woman, expecting Riley to blur past me at the last second to take her out. The smallish thirty-something red head held out both of her palms in my direction as they began to turn bright blue. The same color flashed brilliantly as rings around her neck and her bare arms. I had no idea what her ability could be. I just hoped that Riley would be immune to it.

The muscular man in jean shorts and brown t-shirt raised his long sword over his right shoulder while twisting his body. It looked like a stance I might have seen in a samurai movie. He appeared to be skilled with his weapon. Good. I chose the right opponent for myself, then. I was confident that I could deflect his swing of the deadly blade.

Jada's target seemed much less sure of herself and just held the weapon straight out in front of her. She was a large woman wearing a short jean skirt and thick boots to go with her undersized tank top. Her body bulged out unattractively revealing skin covered with freckles and a sunburn.

The remaining enemy left over for Alexa was roughly her size, and female. She held her bat like she may have been a professional baseball player before all this, wearing short blue shorts and a sleeveless yellow shirt. Her tan skin and long brown hair drew my attention briefly enough to discover that the girl was almost as good looking as my women.

I shifted my attention to the man at the last second. The tactic worked perfectly as Riley shot by me with her bat held sideways with both hands. It struck the unsuspecting gifted girl in the midriff, propelling her backwards off her feet. I couldn't pay much attention to what was happening over there, though, since a sword was being aimed at my precious neck.

I raised my hand to deflect my opponent's blow as I braced my spear shaft under my arm. The sharp metal blade of the samurai blew past my hair as I predicted just when the point of my spear penetrated the man's chest. He was completely shocked by my follow through, and that I was virtually ignoring his sharp decapitating blade. I ran my weapon clear through him and pinned him to the ground beside Riley's foe. He clutched his chest as blood soaked his shirt quickly.

Jada expertly pushed her victim's sword aside with her spear then adjusting the angle to run the point into the woman's oversized gut. The big girl doubled over with an unbelievably loud scream. My dark-skinned companion immediately pulled back on the shaft of her spear to keep it from getting stuck. That was something I should have done instead of running it all the way through my target. I was weaponless because of that mistake.

Alexa's combat prowess, despite her training with Jada, was not impressive. But she tried, bless her heart. Fortunately, her opponent was not that much better. A couple wild swings from each managed to knock the bat from Alexa's hand, though. She quickly took a step backwards to stay out of the path of the pretty girl's next volley. The slender young thing rushed forward to attempt a strike on my wife with an overhead blow. She was soon shocked to find a spearhead exploding from her chest. Jada had quickly come to her friend's aid and delivered what was probably a fatal blow to her second victim within seconds. Jada was a beast and a huge asset to the clan in battle, despite not having any known superpower.

Turning to check on Riley's progress I found her on her back on the ground. Her momentum had likely put her there since she appeared to be unharmed. The blue palmed girl had regained her feet and was debating on whether to attack my fragile friend on the ground, the easy prey, or me as the bigger threat. I made her mind for her by charging.

The red head turned her blue palms at me, rings flashing as evidence of her power in use. I found out firsthand what that power was. An electrical charge shot out of each hand like lightning bolts. I felt intense pain pulse through every part of my body, crippling me instantly, but hopefully not permanently. I dropped to my knees before the small woman as she balled up her fists. Instead of punching my defenseless face, she shook her arms fiercely. I deduced that she was recharging her power. As she opened her palms toward me again, I heard the crack of a baseball bat against her skull. She lost consciousness immediately and fell sideways to the ground. Riley stood behind her with the wooden weapon clutched in both hands.

"Mason!" I heard Alexa scream. Turning toward her, I was happy to discover that the electrical charge was starting to wear off quickly. I could move again. Unfortunately, we had more attackers coming our way. We had beaten four of them, relatively unscathed. But now we had to regroup to face the new threat. This time we were at the disadvantage.

This group had the bearded man in charge, his pistol pointed at my face from less than twenty feet away. To his left was a muscular black woman with a spear, darker skinned than Jada but otherwise her perfect match. On his right was the voluptuous woman without any weapon. Her bronze skin and large breasts were barely covered by the silky green lace dress she wore. Her confidence in herself was profoundly obvious. The last person in the line of attackers was a tall woman carrying a huge fireman's ax. It was painted red and designed to be heaved by the strongest firefighters.

Pop, the bullet released from the barrel of the pistol causing a minor recoil. I raised my hand to deflect it, but not in time to keep from getting hit. I felt my left ear burning as I pulled a dozen bolts from my pocket and tossed them in front of me. My face was turned due to the searing pain in my ear as I swiftly snapped my hand to propel most of the projectiles at the shooter. But he was already dropping to the ground to dodge the effects of my skill. A quick learner he must be. One bolt did contact his forward while another his shoulder, both drawing blood but not near killing him. A third struck the pistol and sent it flying away too far for him to reach. He wasn't reaching for it anyway. Instead, he stared at me with glowing emerald eyes. The same eyes we had witnessed previously on the trance beast. Sure enough, the effect was the same. I went under his spell and lost all motor control of my body.

I could hear Jada beside me ask as if delirious, "What's going on?" I could tell that she was confused by the situation, which was totally unlike her. Then I saw how the confident woman was staring at my friend with a wicked smile on her lovely wide face. That was apparently her ability. She was some kind of confuser, and her focus was entirely on Jada. She no doubt was used to working beside her leader to divide and conquer the enemy.

A familiar blur of black hair and pale skin bolted in front of me with my spear, slamming it down through the heart of the bearded man. Instantly I regained the ability to move. Just in time, too. The heavy fireman's ax was headed right for Riley's head. It was already so close I threw all my skill into the deflection, raising both hands and shouting out. Not only did I succeed in deflecting the blow to miss my clan mate, the change of direction took the tall woman off guard. It hurled her to the ground as she refused to let go of the errant weapon.

Riley dropped to sit her tiny little ass in the grass, totally exhausted by the two speed bursts she had used in such a short time. I didn't see any blood, so I assumed that she was otherwise okay. I would have to make sure that she was not attacked while in that depleted condition.

Jada screamed out as her muscular adversary took advantage of her confused state, jabbing her with the spear. The point only pierced her in the hip, though, because Alexa whacked the shaft downward with her bat at the last second. Otherwise, the weapon could have taken our friend in her beautiful chest.

I charged the spear toting black woman with a battle cry. When she swung the pointy end at me, I dodged the tip and grabbed the shaft with both hands. Using my momentum to overpower the dark woman, I struck her in the face with the pole, possibly breaking her nose. She fell to the ground clutching her face as blood seeped between her fingers.

I lost focus as the confuse-skill woman moved her attention to me. The effect is temporary, though. It ended when Alexa's bat struck the skimpily dressed woman in the temple. She dropped like a sack of potatoes, only not as noisy with her attractive plush body. I quickly refocused to see the remaining four opponent's approach. They hesitated when they saw the carnage we had already caused. That included their dead leader with my spear still protruding straight up toward the sky from his chest. I took the opportunity to snatch up the bearded man's pistol and point it at the rile man's chest while holding another hand forward. There was no longer a reason to hide my deflection skill. I wanted him to know that his rifle was useless against me. Everyone could see the bulging veins in my arms pulsing orange.

"Nobody else has to die here today!" I shouted. "Leave now or we will kill you all."

Jada regains her feet, and her spear to stand beside me, looking more intimidating then she was likely feeling with that hip wound. Riley rose to one knee with the handle of the heavy ax in one hand. I knew that there was no way she could lift the weapon, let alone swing it. Alexa grabs the spear I dropped to fall in line with the rest of us forming our unbeatable foursome.

The broken nose black woman and the tall woman that lost her ax both scurry to stand beside their comrades. I watched as they all inspected the situation trying to determine what to do. I decided to help them figure it out.

"Your man will die first," I said calmly. "Then I will send rocks into everyone's faces so my girls can finish off the rest of you." I raise my aim of the pistol directly at the man's face.

"Okay," the large man finally said. "I'll go." He seemed unsure if the remaining members of his clan would back away with him.

"Leave the rifle," I said.

"No," the man replied. "I need it for protection."

"There won't be anyone to protect if we kill you now," Jada answered for me.

"You still have a spear, a baseball bat, and those two wooden stakes that the blond is holding. I won't strip you of all your weapons. Just enough to make sure you'll leave." I did my best to make it sound non-negotiable. I could see the women then realize that I had planned to let them all go.

"How do I know that you won't shoot us in the back?" the blond asked.

I looked down at their dead leader and remembered his words earlier. "You don't. But what choice do you have?" I saw the man struggle with his decision. "Okay, I promise I won't shoot you. We were not the attackers here. From what I understand, I should just kill your man and take your women. I'm not going to do that, though. Just assure me that you won't return, and I'll let you all live. Now, make the right choice to save these girls of yours. Drop the rifle."

The man was big, and proud, but not stupid. He gently placed the rifle on the ground, turned around and walked away. He didn't even turn to see if the girls would follow him. They didn't.

"What should we do?" the innocent looking brunette holding the spear asked her clan mates. They seemed unsure themselves.

"Do you respect that man?" I ask, gesturing at his large form heading into the sunset on his own.

"John? Yeah, I respect him. He's a good man. Much nicer to me than the other two. But you won."

"Follow John if you want to," I answered. "All of you. If he is a good man, go. You know him. You trust him."

One by one they all gradually went to join the man. When the last one arrived, he turned back to look at me. I couldn't see his face at that distance with the sun declining behind him, but I understood when he raised his hand like he was waving goodbye. He was appreciative of my mercy. Perhaps he was a good man after all. I was never one to mess up another man's situation. I had no hard feelings toward John. I hoped he survives, I honestly did, just as long as he leaves us alone.

"You could have taken his women," Jada stated, not complaining.

"I'm not in a hurry for more sexual competition, thank you," Alexa replied.

"But we could use the numbers," Jada answered.

"That's true," Alexa said. "We barely got through this fight alive. Are you okay, Jada?"

"I'll be fine dear," Jada answered as she put her arm over Alexa's shoulders for support on her injured side. "I just need to get inside and cleaned up. Mason, your ear is bleeding. Are you alright?"

Just then one of the bodies on the ground stirred. It was the voluptuous confuser. Riley rose to her feet and dragged the ax over beside the woman's neck. As the only clan member immune to the woman's ability I appreciated her using what energy she had left.

"What's your name?" I asked, standing over her with the pistol visible in my hand.

"Camilla," she answered, raising to her elbows so she could assess the situation around her. Shock registered on her face when she saw how many of her clan had been defeated. The confidence that she strutted with earlier was now completely absent.

"The few survivors of your clan are heading over the hill. You can catch up to them quickly if you run. Are you feeling well enough to travel?" I ask her as the pain in my ear returns full-force. I ignore it for the time being, resisting the urge to cover it was my hand. I couldn't show any weakness just yet.

"Mason," Riley interrupted. "If I may suggest, Camilla would make an excellent addition to our clan. You have every right to claim her. Perhaps she would choose to join you anyway."

"Is she your type, Mason?" Jada asked.

"I don't claim girls, you know that." I answered Riley and ignored Jada. The injured woman before us was all kinds of sexy. She was fuller figure than I typically liked them, but her sexiness more than overcame that. "Camilla? You are welcome to stay here and get medical attention before making your decision, as long as you promise to behave."

Camilla smiled at me, stood up slowly and adjusted her dress like perhaps she had just stepped out of a limo. My girls all stood ready to attack should she decide to use her ability. "Mason, I would love to get to know you a little better."